'Then you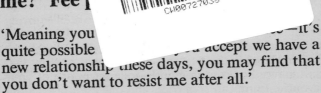
me?' Fee

'Meaning you _____ —it's quite possible _____ you accept we have a new relationship these days, you may find that you don't want to resist me after all.'

Simon's arrogance was outrageous, and Fee gave him a scalding smile, her eyes dark with denial. 'I could never be interested in someone like you. I don't even like you . . .'

Dear Reader

Over the past year, along with our usual wide variety of exciting romances, you will, we hope, have been enjoying a romantic journey around Europe with our Euromance series. From this month, you'll be able to have double the fun and double the passion, as there will now be two Euromance books each month—one set in one of your favourite European countries, and one on a fascinating European island. Remember to pack your passport!

The Editor

Jayne Bauling was born in England and grew up in South Africa. She always wrote but was too shy to show anyone until the publication of some poems in her teens gave her the confidence to attempt the romances she wanted to concentrate on, the first published being written while attending business college. Her home is just outside Johannesburg, a town house ruled by a sealpoint called Ranee. Travel is a major passion; at home it's family, friends, music, swimming, reading and patio gardening.

Recent titles by the same author:

RANSACKED HEART

TRUST
TOO MUCH

BY

JAYNE BAULING

MILLS & BOON LIMITED
ETON HOUSE, 18-24 PARADISE ROAD
RICHMOND, SURREY TW9 1SR

First published in Great Britain 1993
by Mills & Boon Limited

© Jayne Bauling 1993

Australian copyright 1993
Philippine copyright 1993
This edition 1993

ISBN 0 263 78228 X

Set in Times Roman 10 on 11¼ pt.
01-9309-57623 C

Made and printed in Great Britain

CHAPTER ONE

'REMEMBER the lovely parties you used to organise for me when I was little?' Fee Garland smiled affectionately at her stepsister. 'But it's not my birthday now, and I don't know what else you think there is to celebrate. I haven't exactly come home in a blaze of glory. Deepest disgrace is more like it.'

'Don't be so silly,' Babs dismissed the rueful suggestion bracingly, but her sherry-coloured eyes were kind as she glanced up at Fee's pale, sensitive face. 'But if you're worried about what people might say, let them think you've been retrenched. That always gets sympathy.'

But Fee shook her head, unwilling to let herself be misled on that score.

'Don't try to pretend the news hasn't reached Hong Kong, Babs,' she protested shakily, the array of flowers Babs had called her into the lounge to see blurring momentarily before she managed to blink back a rush of tears.

'All right, I have to say that it has, but no one cares, Fee. Everyone here is on your side,' Babs insisted loyally.

'You are, anyway. You always have been,' Fee acknowledged gratefully.

'And you're home, back where you belong. That's reason enough to celebrate,' Babs added determinedly, and Fee had to laugh at the resolution firming the piquant little face beneath a fringe of shiny, streaky hair.

'Who have you invited?' She gave in.

'Oh, the usual crowd. I couldn't remember who all your special friends had been—it's nearly four years, after all—but I did seem to remember that you were once quite friendly with Warren Bates, so I've asked him and he has accepted. As for the rest—oh, masses of people from the old days as well as some new friends you won't know yet.'

Sociable people, Babs and the man she had married had always had scores of friends, Fee recalled as she tried to visualise Warren Bates, the difficulty she experienced in doing so somewhat disconcerting since he had been her very first love.

But the attraction had foundered before anything remotely resembling a relationship could develop, so perhaps her inability to recall his features clearly wasn't so surprising after all, her recollection of the man who had sunk that fragile first romance far more vivid.

'Are your parties still so wild?' she questioned Babs teasingly, her mind returning to present concerns. 'Or has marriage turned you all sedate and sober? The people I knew in Australia were much more conventional than you and your crowd used to be. That's why...'

As she hesitated self-consciously, Babs spoke emphatically. 'Well, we're all still as broad-minded as ever, so you can stop worrying about how people will react to your little adventure if that's what's troubling you.'

'I'm not really worrying, I'm just not exactly looking forward to having a lot of people all looking at me and wondering what really happened. But they'll just have to go on wondering because I don't want to talk about it. I don't have to, except that I'd like to tell *you* that nothing happened and I never did or said anything to make Mr Sheldon think the way he did, or nothing that I'm aware of, anyway.'

'Of course you didn't, darling Fee.' The unquestioning acceptance was warming.

'And if anyone as much as hints otherwise, just you refer him to me.' Charles Sandilands had joined them in time to overhear and he stood in the doorway looking down at his hands and flexing his fingers thoughtfully.

'And if it's a woman, refer her to me,' Babs adjured cheerfully. 'But go and get changed, precious. People will start arriving any minute now, and there's really nothing for you to do down here.'

'Poor little thing,' Fee heard Charles saying as she left the lounge. 'The person I'd really like to get my hands on is Sheldon.'

'The monster,' Babs was agreeing. 'An innocent like Fee!'

'She has changed, though,' Charles sounded a cautionary note. 'I hardly recognised her when we met her at Kai Tak yesterday.'

'Outwardly, but she's still our little Fee,' Babs insisted obstinately.

Combined irritation and amusement banished the threat of tears which had prompted Fee's speedy departure. Everyone, including old friends who had rung up since her return to the hillside house overlooking Repulse Bay, kept calling her 'little', but Babs was the funniest, being six inches shorter than Fee's five-feet-ten.

But Babs *was* five years older, and she had mothered Fee from the moment Jim Garland had brought her and her mother home to his three-year-old daughter, and through all the years afterwards when all they had had to depend on was each other, Jim usually away among his beloved mountains, Angela invariably out pursuing some new man.

Showering hastily, Fee let her mind drift back to Warren Bates, wondering how the teenage attraction between them might have developed if that vile man Simon Rhodes hadn't interfered so unforgivably.

Then, inevitably, her thoughts returned to the situation she had left behind in Australia, with her name

and photo all over the sleazier examples of the popular
Press, Mrs Sheldon disillusioned, Miss Betancourt disappointed, and the famous Vance Sheldon himself in a
towering rage, blaming her and some of his rivals equally
for the way he was suddenly an object of derision all
over the country, and ringing her up at intervals, alter-
nately to vent his anger and to attempt to bully her into
co-operating with his efforts to restore his previously re-
spectable public image by returning to work just as if
nothing had happened.

She hadn't done anything wrong. Fee knew that most
of the time, but the knowledge couldn't alter the fact
that people had been hurt just because she had been so
gullible—so stupidly trusting. She too had been hurt,
mostly in her self-confidence, because she had misread
a situation, and she grieved over the loss of a job she
had liked, but it was the way she shrank from public
attention that had sent her fleeing for home, that
shrinking a legacy from her teens when shyness and her
height combined had made her physically awkward in
company. She had learnt to move gracefully since, but
she still hated attention, and the way the Press had
pursued her had terrified her. Sometimes they had actually seemed to be baying, like some pack of wild
animals, after her blood.

It took a physical effort to wrench her mind free of
the echoes and concentrate on her reflection in the
bedroom mirror. During the years away from Hong
Kong, she had cultivated a softly sophisticated image,
but as she knew only too well, and as Babs had obviously realised, it was only that, an image.

Always slim, the weight she had lost in recent weeks
had left her willowy and over-slender now, with the
shadowy hollows at her temples and beneath her cheekbones giving her a frighteningly fragile look. She just
didn't look tough enough, she reflected unhappily, and,

with the way her fair skin inevitably betrayed her with blushes, how was she going to withstand everyone's curiosity? But she looked composed enough now, her pallor pronounced, emphasising the natural flush of her sensitive lips while her eyes were always shadowy, their blue colour too dark to be identified from a distance, and her graceful black and white skirt worn with a simple sleeveless black top for this warm July night added to the subdued but subtly sophisticated effect. Only her long dark hair, with its tendency to unruly curls unless she wasted time trying to discipline it, provided a contrast.

Having been hearing sounds of people arriving for some time now, she went downstairs reluctantly, apprehension mounting as she reached the hallway and heard the rising swell of sound from the lounge, the noise reminding her a little of those reporters in Australia even though she knew that this wasn't hostile.

And what was she going to do if everyone was as kind as Babs and Charles and the people who had phoned? Everyone had been so nice to her, and it just wasn't doing her any good. She had come home quite instinctively when the pressure had become unbearable, thinking she would be tougher here, among people who had known her since childhood, but it wasn't working. The support and sympathy she was receiving weakened instead of strengthened, and she was furious at finding herself frequently on the verge of tears in response.

'Little Fee should be down in a minute,' Babs was telling someone just inside the lounge.

'Little Fee?' At least there was one person who didn't subscribe to general opinion, and Fee stiffened in shock, instantly recognising the sardonic drawl despite the years gone by since she had last heard it, and in no doubt that nothing complimentary was meant by the contradiction. 'As I recall, she was always a great gangling girl, lurching around all over the place, tipping drinks over people and depositing herself in their laps. I wonder if that's how she caught the great Vance Sheldon? It would need to have been something either original or extreme, with a high-flyer like that.'

'Stop being so vile, Simon,' Babs protested. 'Obviously the man took advantage of the child.'

'Child? She must be—how old?'

'Twenty-two, but . . .'

Fee had turned and begun to creep back up the stairs, so she didn't hear any more, but halfway up she halted and sat down although she was still in full view of anyone who might come out into the hallway. Resolve lifted her chin. She couldn't allow what had happened in Australia to drive her back into the shell from which she had spent painful years struggling to emerge.

But Simon Rhodes! Somehow she had believed that he would have moved on, now that Babs and Charles and, presumably, most of the people who had made up their hedonistic social circle were all respectably married.

Because Simon wouldn't be.

Of course, he and Charles had been friends, she recalled, her shock beginning to recede, and Charles had once been almost as enthusiastic a bachelor as Simon, but how could they have anything in common now? As it was, Simon had tended to become bored with people in general almost as quickly as he tired of the women with whom he involved himself, simply because he was so over-endowed with intelligence.

As for his girlfriends, Hong Kong must be teeming with his rejects by now unless he had changed quite dramatically, Fee reflected with an amusement she had never been able to feel back in the days when Simon Rhodes had always managed to embarrass her in one way or another.

She had detested him then, always uncomfortable in his presence and resenting him for it, although she knew her own inadequacies had been partly responsible for that, having been in her teens and recently grown too tall, too fast to have acquired any sort of grace. But Simon had played his part too, a man whose devastating charm and sophistication had made her feel charmless and gauche by contrast, and whose self-confidence and public success had awed her.

Even then, five or six years ago, Rhodes Properties had reputedly made him a millionaire, and a highly visible one, thanks to his energetic social habits. Rumoured to be a genius, and definitely clever, his womanising contradicted both rumour and fact since most of his short-lived romantic or sexual liaisons featured women of distinctly limited intellect, although some great female minds were also said to have succumbed to his undeniable charm.

He was also known to be temperamental, and Fee, who substituted selfish and superficial for all the more popular descriptions, had twice found herself on the receiving end of his temper, the first occasion being when he had rejected one woman in favour of another at one of Babs' parties, the memory still capable of making her cringe. Fee needed to think a minute before recalling that the woman had been one Ismay Compton. Oh, she had been so naïve, raging at him like that after over-hearing his coolly ruthless rejection and witnessing Ismay's tearful departure.

'How can you be so brutal?' she had stormed at him on emerging from the downstairs room in which they had installed the computer which, infuriatingly, Simon had helped her and Babs to choose after the latter had decided that Fee needed one at home in order to assist the commercial course she was taking at school and had somehow got the money out of Jim Garland. 'Can't you see she loves you, you horrible man?'

'Quite possibly she does, but love doesn't last, as you'll find out for yourself, darling.' Clearly hovering between amusement and the irritation that was making his eyes glitter, Simon had paused, examining her critically. 'Although not from me, I'm afraid, if that's what you're hanging around in the hope of, as I find teeny-boppers a singularly unprepossessing species. But see me when you've grown up and acquired some looks and experience, and I might be prepared to reconsider.'

In those days, she had lacked the composure to correct his arrogant assumption, rage and embarrassment rendering her inarticulate, and she had followed Ismay's example and fled.

Now a nervous little laugh escaped her as she recalled the other incident—that to which Simon Rhodes had been referring—but anger followed. She thought it had happened four years ago, about a year after she had attacked him over his rejection of Ismay Compton. There had been a barbecue but it had rained and everyone had gone inside—except for her and Warren Bates. The two of them had been looking shyly at each other at school for ages, and she had finally found the courage to invite him to the barbecue. They had been so tentative, nervous of each other but reluctant to become part of the crowd indoors, both jumping with embarrassment when their hands touched before deciding that they liked the feeling, linking their fingers, smiling self-consciously at each other.

It was at that precise moment that Simon had stepped out into the softly falling rain, probably bored by the company inside. He had looked at them, standing there holding hands, and then Fee had seen the icy anger gathering in his eyes.

'You're not part of the regular circuit, are you?' he had addressed Warren contemptuously. 'These parties are closed affairs.'

'I invited him,' Fee flared heatedly as Warren snatched his hand away, sulky and scarlet-faced.

'And who invited you, darling?' Simon retorted coolly. 'This is an adult party.'

'I happen to live here!' She had been so angry that for once she'd been able to address him without any self-conscious stammering.

'Which entitles you to what precisely?' He had remained coldly angry.

'Babs——'

'Babs is broke as usual, so this isn't her party. Charles Sandilands and I happen to be financing it, and we put a ban on gatecrashers and juveniles, so get rid of him and make yourself scarce.'

Then he had turned abruptly and gone inside again. Nothing Fee could say or do had succeeded in soothing Warren's wounded pride, and he had departed without re-entering the house, leaving her to rejoin the adults defiantly, seething with fury as she met Simon's eyes.

'I thought I told you to make yourself scarce? Evidently love's young dream is more amenable to taking a hint than you are,' he suddenly commented with a slight edge to his voice, addressing her from a chair close to the table from which she had just helped herself to a glass of wine.

'Hint? I hate you,' she had muttered furiously. 'Just because you're in a bad mood about something——'

Fee had never been sure what had happened then. Rage was choking her and all her co-ordination seemed to desert her and as she tried to prevent the accident, too late because it had already happened and a startled Simon was drenched in wine, either she or the floor had tilted and she had ended up sprawling over him.

The subsequent explosion of temper had shocked everyone present, their laughter dying as Simon's considerable sense of humour had deserted him for once, while Fee could only stand there stammering, dying of humiliation as he had expressed himself uninhibitedly on the subject of her clumsiness specifically and the presence of adolescents at adult parties in general.

Babs had eventually dragged her out of the room and comforted her, and after that day Fee had taken pains to remain hidden in her bedroom whenever he was around. That period hadn't lasted long, though, as she had just passed her final exams, and the increasingly restless urge to discover the world beyond Hong Kong that had kept her and two schoolfriends diligently saving every dollar they earned over several years at their part-time jobs on supermarket tills had at least seen them heading for Australia.

Now she was home, and Simon Rhodes was still around, as insensitive as ever.

Fee stood up again and began to descend the stairs, suddenly eager to confront Simon and show him that she was no longer the gauche teenager of four years ago, bereft of any defiance against his contempt. What she had overheard had first embarrassed and then angered her, but now her anticipation was unexpectedly mixed with an odd pleasure. It was just ironic that his unsympathetic attitude should be giving her this sort of strength, when everyone else's kindness had merely succeeded in weakening her.

To her satisfaction, Simon was standing just inside the lounge, close to the door, apparently listening to the breathless chatter of one of the loveliest women Fee had ever seen—only apparently, because his eyes, of a blue that was utterly different from the blue of hers, were roaming the room and lingering typically every time they came to rest on an attractive woman.

Fee felt a surge of sheer excitement as she observed him, like the exhilaration of an adrenalin-rush, but she knew it wasn't really personal. Simon just had that effect on people generally. In his presence, women sparkled and men were on their mettle, upping the level of their conversation, becoming wittier and cleverer.

He was tall, probably over six feet, and preposterously handsome, exactly as she remembered him although he was in his thirties now and his lifestyle ought to be telling; but there were no signs of dissipation that she could see so far, only the same arrogant enjoyment just touched with a contradictory trace of boredom. Leanly built, he looked elegant but subtly powerful in his immaculate smart-casual clothes, and superbly healthy, skin as tanned and light hair as naturally sun-bleached as ever because, as Fee recalled, he played as enthusiastically as he worked, regularly disappearing to exotic and glamorous pleasure-spots all over the world, usually taking a woman along with him.

The beautifully shaped head turned as if he had sensed her approach and for a second his glance was alert yet simultaneously indifferent, and she remembered how ruthless he could be in his dismissal of people, both men and women, who failed to interest him.

'May I lurch past you, please?' she requested limpidly, with a smile for his companion.

'Fee.' As recognition lit those bright, warm blue eyes, it was as if all his natural vitality blazed up into full life, touching all those around him, and yet seconds later his expression was hardening, eyes narrowing in cynical appraisal. 'And look at you, all grown up and home from the wars.'

'The lynch mob is more like it. How are you, Simon? Don't worry, I'm quite safe without a drink.' She showed him her empty hands and gave the woman beside him another smile. 'Hello, I don't think I know you, do I?'

'You heard,' Simon realised softly, the cynical look vanishing and his slow smile of wicked enjoyment revealing perfectly white and even teeth. 'And you're cross with me, but I refuse to apologise as eavesdroppers only ever hear the truth and you were a physical threat to everyone in your vicinity—although, looking at you now and guessing where the glamour comes from, I think that these days I might find one of the collisions in which you specialised somewhat more exciting than I did back then.'

Then, without giving her time to react, he introduced her and Loren Kincaid to each other. A few years older than Fee, Loren was small but exquisitely endowed with perfectly proportioned curves, as well as a shining cap of jet-black hair and huge violet eyes. She had been looking insecure, Fee had noticed, a familiar state among Simon's women when his gaze started travelling, but now her rosebud mouth relaxed into a genuinely friendly smile, presumably because she had decided that Fee wasn't to be regarded as a rival for this glamorous, gorgeous but incorrigibly restless man.

'This party is to welcome you home, isn't it? I think you did the right thing, Fee, coming back,' Loren assured her with earnest goodwill. 'You'll feel safe here.'

'Why in the world should she want to feel safe?' Simon expressed exaggerated astonishment, his gaze probing as it swivelled to Fee. 'It did occur to me that your stepsister might have a point when she was loyally insisting that you'd been taken advantage of, but that was while I was still visualising the old Fee. Now that I see you, I refuse to believe it. Quite clearly you've learnt to take care of yourself and are safe anywhere. Congratulations. You had your fun, pulling one of Australia's top financiers and then leaving him looking a total prat into the bargain. I imagine you've come home to celebrate.'

'I didn't pull——' Fee stopped herself, realising that she was about to sound like the gauche eighteen-year-old she had been when last she had seen him, because that was how he had momentarily made her feel again.

'I know you've never minded it, Simon, but not everyone enjoys seeing their name all over the newspapers, and having lies written about them, and reporters in the garden shouting questions at them every time they open the door to try and go out and buy milk.'

He shrugged indolently. 'No, I've never minded, since just about everything written about me is true. I've never had anything to hide.'

'Or be ashamed of?' Fee prompted drily.

'You're not ashamed of what you did, are you?' Simon laughed. 'Don't be——'

'I didn't *do* anything,' she interrupted, eyes blazing as she realised that, probably alone among the people here tonight, he believed that she had been as actively responsible as Vance Sheldon for the scandal that had entertained all Australia in recent weeks. 'Thanks, Loren, I know I'll be safe here. Excuse me, please, I'd better go and say hello to everyone, especially since this party is supposed to be for me.'

Simon laughed and said something in a low voice to Loren as she left them, trying to make her movements slow and even as it was haste and hesitation which had caused the physical disasters of her teens. The trouble was that somehow Simon had made her feel like a teenager again, all hot and bothered, and yet angry too, especially now that she kept catching him watching her with idly speculative interest as she moved around the room, renewing her acquaintance with old friends and being introduced to strangers.

But at least he hadn't been kind!

As she had feared, everyone else was very kind, the more tactful pretending that there was nothing out of the ordinary about her homecoming, a few embarrassing her by referring openly to what had happened, and all firmly convinced of her innocence.

It made Simon Rhodes unique. Everyone else still saw her as the child she had been when she had left Hong Kong, Fee realised ruefully, although she wasn't sure she found Simon's view of her any more flattering.

At least Warren Bates ought to see her as an adult, having once been romantically interested in her, she reflected wryly, finally placing the young man who was approaching her now, and perhaps as the sort of adult she really was, without making any of Simon's cynical and gratuitous assumptions.

Once Warren had seemed the most beautiful male creature in the world, and the green eyes with their thick fringe of black lashes still stirred her, but his personality seemed mediocre and somewhat repressed now. He spoke in polite platitudes, only becoming human when he mentioned Simon.

'I saw you speaking to him when you came in. The man is a swine. I didn't know he'd be here.' His tone implied that he wouldn't have come had he done so.

'Oh, he and Charles are old friends. Their circle doesn't seem to have changed much over the years, even if marriage has given most of the women new surnames,' Fee laughed. 'That redhead over there used to be Ismay Compton, for instance. She must have got over Simon if she can bear to be here. You have to give him credit for managing to stay friends with most of his ex-girlfriends.'

'You seem very interested in him.' Warren sounded resentfully suspicious and, remembering how Simon had once treated him, Fee was contrite.

'Never mind Simon, tell me what you've been doing all these years... Only give me a minute first, please? I think Charles and Babs have forgotten to put any soft drinks out and I'm still too dehydrated from the flight yesterday to risk alcohol. Don't go away.'

To Fee's surprise, Loren Kincaid followed her into the kitchen.

'You mustn't mind Simon being so nasty to you,' she told her kindly, examining the drinks Fee was extracting from the fridge and finding nothing of interest. 'It's just his way.'

'Oh, I'm used to him,' Fee assured her, touched.

'I'm sure he knows you're an innocent victim, really. Everyone who knows you says so, and it's obvious from the newspaper stories—even to me, and Simon says I'm an airhead. But I'd better get back to him.' She laughed bravely. 'There are too many attractive women around for my liking. He really is awful!'

And in the end Loren would get hurt, just like all the others, Fee reflected drily. Simon was impossible.

Carefully, she carried a tray laden with a variety of non-alcoholic drinks into the large, elegantly furnished lounge and put it down, helping herself to a glass of mineral water as Warren Bates rejoined her. Suddenly she felt tired, and a little depressed, and she glanced longingly out towards the patio beyond the sliding glass doors which stood open.

'I don't think I'm really a party animal,' she confided. 'Let's go outside for a minute, and you can tell me all your news. Or are you with someone?'

He wasn't, so they sat on the stairs leading down to the swimming-pool, talking about simple things that didn't hurt, and Fee found herself telling him how the house still belonged to her father.

'It seemed practical for Charles to move in when he and Babs married because they'll be going to England once his stint in charge of his father's factories here is up. He used to tell people he was the modern equivalent of a remittance man——'

She broke off, hearing someone else behind them.

'This isn't very sociable of you, Fee,' Simon Rhodes said mockingly. 'Especially when you're the guest of honour. Or do you intend to renew your acquaintance with each of us separately? You never much liked crowds, I remember. In that case, your time is up, Bates, and it's my turn.'

His tone held an undercurrent that was obscurely significant, and Warren glared at him as he stood up, but he wasn't old enough or sufficiently sure of himself to accept it as a challenge. Fee felt vaguely disappointed in him. She had learnt to fight back, however unsure of herself she might feel inwardly, so why hadn't Warren?

But simple kindness and the sensitive awareness that any reference to his previous encounter with Simon Rhodes would discomfit him dictated that she wait until he had departed, muttering, before saying tartly, 'Talk about *déjà vu*! What have you got against him?'

One of the strangest things about Simon was the way his presence made people feel more alive, she reflected, her tiredness vanishing as he took Warren's place beside her. He seemed to radiate a kind of energy that affected everyone around him. It was a visible thing, a vibrant blaze that came from within, probably merely a manifestation of his sheer vitality, and highly unfair, because it should have been a sign of great goodness or spirituality, and there was nothing remotely saintly or inspiring about him.

'Renewing an old acquaintance, or resuming a relationship, Fee?' Simon settled himself comfortably.

'There wasn't any relationship to renew,' she retorted resentfully. 'Thanks to you.'

'And you're wondering what you missed out on?' he guessed wickedly. 'I suppose his youth is what appeals to you after that old man you were involved with in Australia.'

Fee gave him a furious look as the soft light streaming from the house above them showed her that he was only half joking.

'I suppose it's inevitable that you should think like that, given your own history, but I think I'm a little more discriminating than you are, Simon,' she snapped.

'Where Bates is concerned? Or Sheldon?' Simon returned mockingly, his lips quirking as he cast her a quick, curious glance. 'I'm intrigued. Do you really prefer old men, sweetheart, or is it some power game you're playing, with the final denunciation written into the play before it even gets underway?'

Fee knew he was a cynic, but it was still disconcerting to realise he could believe such things of her.

'There was nothing between me and Mr Sheldon,' she insisted tightly.

'Oh, come on, darling. You were in that hotel room together, weren't you?' Simon laughed. 'All right, it was probably going too far to suspect someone like you of deliberately setting the guy up—not that it doesn't sound as if he richly deserved it—but why are you so defensive about it all?'

'You actually think it's funny, don't you?' Fee realised furiously. 'Why aren't you disgusted?'

'Why the hell should I be?' Simon laughed. 'You've obviously benefited from the experience, and we all have to sow a few wild oats, if I may be utterly trite.'

'They're hardly still wild oats at your age,' she retaliated, grasping eagerly at the chance to change the subject.

'I'm not quite ready for a retirement resort yet. Thirty-three,' he drawled lazily.

'As I said, at your age,' Fee emphasised sweetly, and added, 'Loren is nice.'

'Beautiful,' Simon agreed, infuriatingly relaxed. 'But none too bright.'

'Bright enough to have noticed your roving eye,' she asserted waspishly.

'I'm not in any need of advice about my love life, thanks, Fee.' Abruptly there was a slight but audible edge to his voice, cool and sharp.

'What has love got to do with it?' she wondered innocently.

'Everything. I love women.'

The statement, so outrageous and so simple, silenced Fee for several seconds. It was the absolute, unadorned truth, she realised, and any further explanation of his playboy habits would be superfluous. Simon loved women, so much that he was incapable of loving just one for any length of time, if in fact he ever actually loved them as individuals.

'You never used to state the obvious,' she taunted softly.

'You seemed in some doubt,' Simon countered derisively. 'But as I've said, it's *your* love life that intrigues me right now. Tell me about Sheldon. Were you his personal assistant?'

'I hadn't risen quite that high yet. I was assistant to his real assistant, but the position was supposed to lead to promotion eventually.'

Her bright, tender mouth drooped as she recalled the trouble Miss Betancourt had taken, grooming her to be her replacement when she retired in a few years' time. All for nothing——

'You must have counted it worth sacrificing since you were prepared to incur Sheldon's anger by making the thing public knowledge,' Simon cut into her reflections unsympathetically.

She hadn't had any choice, unless she had been prepared to let Vance Sheldon rape her, since the Press, so much more cynically suspicious than she, had been on the spot, ready and waiting, eager for drama.

She flung Simon an angrily resentful look as she picked up her glass from beside her on the step and took a sip of mineral water.

'I don't want to talk about it,' she stated tautly. 'As everyone knows, he fired me or I resigned, depending on which version of the story you believe, so I've got more important things to think about, like finding myself another job, and somewhere to live, and a car.'

'Here in Hong Kong?' he probed.

'I think so, yes.' She couldn't face going back, although she wasn't about to reveal her vulnerability by admitting it. 'Hong Kong is my home. I belong here.'

Simon sent her a glance sparkling with mockery. 'And you'll be able to behave as badly as you like within a circle where no one will judge you and make a scandal of it as they seem to have done in Australia, since we all behaved equally badly most of the time. It's just strange, or perhaps ironic, that you had to go away to become one of us. I like the change, but what happened to the old Fee? Is there any of her left there inside the sophisticated packaging?'

'There's hardly likely to be, is there? I'm twenty-two, but on her behalf, since she could never stand up for herself or answer back... Yes, you do all behave badly, especially at these parties, I remember, so why shouldn't I?' As she spoke, Fee stood up, still holding her glass, looking down into it for a moment before pouring the remainder of its contents into his lap. 'Last time was an accident, Simon. This was deliberate, in case you're in any doubt. Sorry it had to be in the region of both your intellect and your emotions.'

Simon swore, following it with such absolute silence that she couldn't resist the temptation to look back as she gained the patio. His shoulders shook, and then she heard his laughter.

'Oh, you were right, you truly do belong here.' His amused voice drifted up to her. 'You're one of our own. Welcome home, Fee.'

Fleetingly, it gave rise to apprehension which subsided when he made no move to detain her.

She hadn't felt this good in weeks, Fee realised. The only disconcerting thing about it was that it should be Simon Rhodes, of all people, who had revived her fighting spirit.

CHAPTER TWO

SIGHING, Fee let the newspaper fall to the ground beside the sun-lounger on which she was reclining. None of the positions advertised was exactly inspiring, and likely to add to her difficulties was her intention to be scrupulously discriminating in her choice of boss this time around. She wasn't risking another Vance Sheldon—never again! On the whole, she was inclined to think that putting her name down with an employment agency might be her best bet. For safety's sake, she might even opt for temping, she decided, unless she found the perfect boss.

The sun had set but darkness had yet to fall, and it was one of those sultry, gently steaming July evenings she remembered so well from years gone by, the stillness of the air giving all Hong Kong's island side a dreaming aspect, and yet down in town among the gracefully rearing spires the movement and noise would be as vibrant as ever, equally so over on Kowloonside. But not up here, high above Repulse Bay, blue-white jewel set amid gentle emerald slopes. It was silent here, and soothing.

Her mood of exhilaration hadn't lasted long after she had tipped her drink into Simon's lap two evenings ago. She had locked herself into her bedroom, ignoring the people who came and knocked at intervals and eventually falling into the first truly dreamless sleep she had been granted in weeks, despite the sounds of carousing downstairs—because Loren Kincaid had been right. She felt safe here.

She had no idea how or if Simon had explained the state of his elegant trousers to anyone, and she hadn't enquired, beginning to be embarrassed by her behaviour since such a confrontational attitude was alien to her nature.

A sound from the high patio above her made her withdraw her gaze from the sparkling clarity of the swimming-pool, and there was the subject of her thoughts, Simon Rhodes, carrying his jacket and coming down the stairs towards her. A pang of purely aesthetic appreciation assailed her as she watched him. He moved with such grace and leashed power, and was so beautifully formed, so truly physically perfect in every way that she could only be profoundly grateful that she would never be one of the legion of women who loved him, because how did anyone ever get over such a man?

'Charles isn't home yet,' she informed him casually, resolutely deciding to ignore the fact that the mere sight of him made her feel challenged in some obscure way. 'But Babs is somewhere inside.'

'Thank you, she sent me out to join you.' Simon stood beside her sun-lounger, looking down at her and then at the pool on her other side, a wicked gleam appearing in his eyes. 'I am so tempted, Fee, after the drenching I received at your hands the other night.'

'Don't you dare! And you're exaggerating... I'm sorry I threw my drink over you, Simon.' But although she had begun to be ashamed of herself, Fee's eyes still sparkled at the memory, and her voice refused to emerge as demurely as she wanted it to, a quiver betraying her as she added, 'I don't usually behave like that. I don't know what got into me.'

'A devil, of course, and it's looking out of your eyes right now, so I suppose I ought to keep my distance. But all right, I'll forgive you since it was probably due,' he conceded magnanimously, ignoring the advice he had just given himself and pulling a matching chair closer to her lounger before seating himself. 'I shouldn't have bawled you out in front of everyone the way I did that other time.'

'No, you shouldn't,' she agreed tartly, still capable of flushing at the memory, and deciding against asking what had got into *him* on that occasion.

'So how is our innocent victim, as Loren keeps insisting you are? I believe she thinks she invented the phrase all by herself.'

'If you're so scathing about people's intellectual limitations behind their backs—and to their faces, now I think of it, because she said you'd called her an airhead—why do you go out with such bimbos?' Fee flared, incensed on Loren's behalf.

Simon wore his most arrogant expression. 'Because they don't try so hard to be clever, whereas half-bright women keep trying to be cleverer than they are and it bores me because I see through them.'

'God, have you any idea how inhibited your intolerance must make people when you can't even be bothered to hide it? I'll be frightened to open my mouth now,' Fee claimed tempestuously.

'You don't count,' Simon said rudely, with an indifferent glance at her mouth before noticing the newspaper she had discarded and observing at which page it was open. 'Looking for...what did you tell me? A home, a car and a job? In fact, we may be able to help you with the first. Rhodes Properties are mainly commercial and industrial, but we have recently added a division dealing with residential, and it's turning out to be a paying concern with land here so scarce, and rents for ground-floor apartments as high as you choose to make them when everyone is so nervous of a cut in electricity putting lifts out of order... But haven't you considered staying here? The house still belongs to your father, doesn't it?'

'Yes.' Fee glanced up at the green-tiled roof, a sort fairly common in Hong Kong. 'But it's everyone's home really, for all of us to come back to. If you must know, I want to get away from Babs and Charles because if I'm not independent they're likely to go on treating me like a baby forever.'

And because she wasn't a natural fighter, she was afraid she might be tempted to settle for the easy option and let them, Fee supplemented silently, but she wasn't about to confide that much to Simon. For some reason it was important that he shouldn't guess how much of the old, uncertain Fee still existed.

He was sending a lazily amused smile across the space between them.

'They must be blind. It's definitely a very adult Fee who has come home to us.' Pausing, he observed her complicated reaction to the meaningful tone before digressing, 'Your father is still mountaineering, isn't he?'

'In a sense. I think he's part of a movement to clear old base-camp sites of litter all over Pakistan and Nepal, now that the problem has been realised, so he's giving something back, which is nice. Mountains are all he has ever cared about; all the pleasure he has had has come from them,' Fee acknowledged the kind of single-minded selfishness that had long since ceased to perturb her.

'Lucky he had the means to indulge himself.' Simon referred to the private fortune Jim Garland had spent in pursuit of his obsession.

'He usually remembered to keep us supplied with money to live on, and he did buy this house,' Fee reminded him loyally.

'And dumped you in it when you were a baby. Wasn't there some near-scandal about that?' Simon frowned.

She laughed. 'After my mother died when I was two. She'd never properly recovered from some complication at my birth because it happened somewhere remote in the Himalayas, with no doctors for hundreds of miles. The nannies he left me with here kept walking out, and someone found out and threatened to take him to court if I wasn't looked after better, so he married Angela. She had Babs, and nowhere to live and no money—poor Babs doesn't even know who her father was—so it worked out quite well when he was home, only Angela likes lots of attention and a man to be around all the time, and he kept telling her horror stories about my mother's trials to discourage her because he didn't want her with him in the mountains.'

Simon shook his head. 'You girls must have had an even more chaotic childhood than I did. My various step-parents and unofficial aunts and uncles kept changing, but they were there. Angela wasn't often, was she?'

Fee shook her head.

'She's an incurable romantic, always out looking. But Babs looked after me, and when we were older we looked after each other. I shiver when I think about it some-times, though,' she added in a hushed voice. 'Once I got pneumonia and Babs couldn't make the doctor's recep-tionist understand her, and another time it was cold and she decided we should have a hot meal. She was only ten and she burnt her hand badly, and I was frantic; I didn't know what to do...'

'God, it's a horror story.' Simon sounded unusually thoughtful and he studied her expression for a moment. 'People shouldn't get married. Jim and Angela have never bothered with a divorce, have they? Angela was home last year, but then she met someone on his way to take up a contract job somewhere—Jakarta, I think—and she took off with him. But you're a big girl now and don't need anyone to take care of you, as you've just demonstrated by walking out on your lover in Australia and not even bothering to be discreet about it, all in the fine tradition of your odd family.'

Fee didn't think she had taken care of herself at all successfully, considering the humiliation she had suffered as a consequence of her own stupid naïveté, and, while she loved her family, she had no intention of following in any of their footsteps. Her dreams were conventional, of a husband who came home to her and children she would care for herself.

'You would believe that was the way it was,' she taunted sharply. 'It may interest you to know that absolutely no one else does.'

'As we've agreed, that's because the fools all still see you as the child they remember. But you and I both know you're not. You grew up in a sexually sophisticated milieu and it was only a matter of time before you adopted our mores. Welcome to the real, adult world, darling. It's a pleasure to know you—or it will be.'

Fee just managed not to look startled. For a moment it had almost sounded as if he was flirting with her, the way he did with other women, but surely that was impossible? Not Simon. Not with her!

'You're wrong! About the Australian business, I mean.' Her dark blue eyes flashed as she dismissed the ridiculous idea. 'But I don't care what you think.'

'That's the spirit,' he commended her insouciantly. 'Never explain yourself, never make excuses, never mind what people say and think. Incidentally, Charles was telling me on the phone earlier that you weren't finding the job market too promising. That's why I'm here. I might just have something for you if the position of assistant to Sheldon's assistant entailed what I imagine it did. There's a woman who's leaving Rhodes whose position you might be able to fill, although why she has to take off so inconveniently is beyond me. Her excuse is so stupidly irrational that I refuse to dignify it by calling it a reason.'

Fee's anger subsided and she looked at him hopefully, aware that Rhodes Properties' reputation was excellent, but then rare pride stirred.

'I don't need you and Charles to arrange my life for me, thank you very much, Simon,' she asserted caustically. 'I'm quite capable of finding a job for myself, and, considering how scathing you've been about other people's failure to realise that I'm not a helpless baby any more, I'd have expected you to tell him to go to hell when he asked you.'

The smile Simon gave her was biting. 'Oh, definitely not a helpless baby. A spitting cat is more like it, and I do mean the wild kind. Charles didn't exactly ask me——'

'No, but I bet he hinted like mad and you felt obliged to come up with something because he's a friend and you men have this stupid buddy-code about helping each other out,' she accused tempestuously. 'I don't mind Charles interfering so much, because he's family, but I don't really even know you except as his friend, so don't try to make a charity of me. I won't accept it.'

Simon was still smiling at her, derisively now, but something flickering at the back of his eyes seemed to suggest that she had either angered or offended him.

'No, you don't really know me at all, Fee, if you can imagine I'd make you my good deed for the day,' he drawled mockingly. 'I've no objection to doing Charles a favour, but not if it's at the expense of anything to do with Rhodes Properties. Assuming you're interested in the position, I'll only appoint you if you're qualified for it. Right now, I have to say I have my doubts, if you're stupid enough to believe anything else.'

Fee had always been flexible, seeing no point in clinging obstinately to an idea once it was proved to have no foundation, but something in Simon's attitude was angering her, and her apology carried a distinct trace of acid.

'Sorry! I was forgetting that first and foremost you're a hard-headed businessman. Blame it on the way people talk about you. Everyone is so riveted by the *social* side of your life. But I should have remembered that Rhodes Properties is the one thing you truly take seriously—far more seriously than you do your famous love life.'

Simon shrugged dismissively. 'Since, properly administered and maintained, property not only increases in value but is the one thing that actually lasts. Love doesn't.'

Irrationally, since she had already known he believed something of the sort, it intensified her anger.

'It might, properly cared for... It does, if people work at it, I'm sure.'

'Who has got that much emotional energy?' Simon retorted cynically. 'I haven't. You haven't either, obviously, or you'd still be in Australia with Sheldon. I'm assuming you were the lazy one, given the particular nature of your very public break-up.'

'Love didn't come into that,' Fee snapped, for once mercifully undistressed by the reference, too fascinated by his attitude and driven by some compulsion to try and understand it. 'I suppose you're so cynical because you've never seen anyone working at a relationship. You called my family life a horror story and my family odd, but you had all those step-parents and so-called aunts and uncles coming and going——'

Simon's laughter stopped her. It was genuinely amused, but there was something hard in his eyes, denial or rejection, lending them the brilliance of diamonds.

'Forget it, Fee, I dealt with all that years ago—not that it required much in the way of effort. There were no villains or victims, just a lot of nice, normal people, all coming and going, as you've mentioned. I never expected anything else.'

'So you were never disappointed,' Fee taunted softly, furious at the way he made her feel so naïvely idealistic.

'Don't try to analyse me, darling,' he advised her with idle indifference. 'You're sure to get it all wrong.'

'Yes, I suppose you flatter yourself you're a madly complex, superior being, whereas men are actually the simpler sex, as every woman knows,' she claimed with a swift, blistering smile.

But she didn't really believe there was anything simple about him, while Vance Sheldon had taught her that some men were devious and not to be trusted.

'Oh, I've always thought of myself as fairly uncomplicated,' Simon offered easily.

'All right!' Irritated by his lack of co-operation with her attempts to comprehend him, Fee gave it up since he so clearly didn't want to be understood. 'I accept it. You're just a simple, single-minded businessman and Rhodes Properties is the only thing in the world that really means anything to you, the only lasting relationship you'll ever have.'

'Well, don't sound so disapproving about it,' he adjured her amusedly, but then he frowned. 'At least I'm never bored by work.'

After a moment she decided he wasn't implying anything personal, and she considered his words, which had allowed her a glimpse of the isolation that his intellect must impose. Rhodes Properties probably provided him with his only real intellectual stimulation, and somehow that struck her as sad, making her wonder if he was ever consciously lonely.

But the amused way in which he had brushed off all her attempts to understand him better deterred her from probing further. Maybe he enjoyed being misunderstood, or perhaps there was nothing there *to* understand. Hadn't she always thought of him as superficial? So why this instinctive urge to look for hidden depths? He had given her no cause to believe any existed.

Suppressing the strange fancies that had prompted her, she ventured cautiously, 'If you're serious about having a job for me, I do have a testimonial.'

Miss Betancourt had insisted.

'For what it's worth, and my word is worth a lot, I'm going to give you a reference since Mr Sheldon is still refusing, and exercising your legal rights there is going to take time. I'll make it clear that both he and I have found your work entirely satisfactory, and there's no need to mention anything else, although I'm afraid anyone who has heard the story is bound to wonder; but it's time you stopped blaming yourself so much. Your only fault was that you were too trusting. Finding yourself his only guest at the races should have made you suspicious; it's what alerted the Press... But there's no point in worrying about it now, and you can also stop worrying about the other people concerned. Mrs Sheldon isn't nearly as shocked as you imagine, since she has never had many illusions about her husband.'

The pen Simon removed from the pocket of the lightweight jacket he had dropped on to another chair was a ball-point, but the most expensive in a range that had left left Fee wondering, when she had once seen an advertisement, what sort of person would spend such a fortune on something so utilitarian.

'A Miss Sung-Li is head of Personnel. Ring her on Monday, but not first thing, because I'll need to have a word with her, and if she thinks you're qualified for the job she'll make appointments for both of us to interview you.'

Fee regarded him levelly.

'If you're really not just being kind, because I'm Charles's sister-in-law——'

'I'm never kind,' Simon interrupted distastefully, following it with a complicated smile.

'No, you're not,' she conceded tartly, accepting that her assumption had been a stupid one, and jumping slightly as he handed her the card on which he had just scribbled the name and number she would need and their fingers brushed, Simon's warm and hard. 'I don't suppose you've ever done a single altruistic action in your life.'

An amusedly reflective gleam appeared in his eyes.

'Strangely enough, I used to flatter myself that I might have, once, and I'm not at all sure I won't yet live to regret it, or else find it rebounding on me in some way.' Then the thoughtful expression vanished as he paused, warm blue eyes glinting as they lingered on her face a moment before skimming her slender body and the length of her legs, pale because her fair skin couldn't take much sun, but smooth and slim. 'Why did you take up office work? You could have been a model. You're not strictly beautiful, but then many models aren't when you see what lies under the tricks they perform with make-up.'

'And you've seen hundreds?' Fee taunted.

'Not so many really. I generally prefer small, curvy women myself.'

'But not because they make you feel protective,' she guessed acidly.

'Hell, no,' he confirmed, drawling slightly. 'I like a woman who can take care of herself, stand up for herself, and the sassy little ones usually can.'

He would. Fee supposed that was partly why he had never appealed to her personally. She knew it wasn't fashionable, but she dreamed of the sort of man who would take care of her while refraining from the sort of babying that people like Babs and Charles offered her — not that she couldn't look after herself generally, of course, despite the self-doubt she had suffered since misreading Vance Sheldon's intentions.

'So you're able to feel superior without having to be protective at the same time,' she mocked.

'Everyone is the same height in bed.' Simon was dismissive. 'Out of it, your height would have made you ideal for ramp work, especially now that that incredible grace has replaced your clumsiness, so how come you never considered modelling?'

'Mainly because I don't like a lot of people looking at me,' she vouchsafed shortly.

'Why not?' His eyes were bright with interest.

'I once had an unpleasant experience,' she began pointedly, and saw his face harden.

'You've had all the apology you're getting, Fee, so don't go on about it,' he advised her ruthlessly, before smiling. 'All the same it's a pity... Nice legs too. You can wear shorts and miniskirts. Usually the women who do definitely shouldn't... Here's Babs.'

He stood up to go and help Babs who had appeared on the patio with a tray of drinks, leaving Fee blushing and confused. His manner had begun to perplex her, nowhere near as boredly indifferent, occasionally teasing and sometimes rude as it had been in her teens, for which she was grateful; but his odd, brief forays into the realm of what might loosely be termed flirtation were disconcerting, mainly because they were so inconsistent. She had to suppose that they arose out of mere habit, simply because he was such a chronic flirt, programmed to a certain automatic pattern of behaviour in female company, whether the women concerned interested him or not. He probably didn't even realise he was doing it, and would be startled if she ever flirted back, she reflected wryly.

She glanced down at her denim shorts and pretty white cotton top and found confirmation of her suspicion; despite the air of sophistication she had managed to acquire over the years, but which she frequently tended to forget she possessed simply because she still *felt* so unsophisticated, she was sure she was devoid of the sort of glamour common to the women who attracted Simon.

Mercifully, her face had cooled by the time he and Babs arrived on the pool-deck, although Simon threw her an amused look as if he had discerned the trend of her recent thoughts. Fee prevented herself fidgeting self-consciously and managed to keep her expression composed, relieved when he seemed disinclined to make any further personal comments.

Charles arrived home from work a few minutes later and came out to join them, but Simon stood up to leave as soon as he had finished his drink.

'A date?' Charles enquired interestedly.

'Work.'

Charles shook his head incredulously. 'When are you ever going to ease up, man?'

Simon shrugged. 'It's my choice, Charles.'

'On a Friday night? And with the lovely Loren no doubt waiting for you!'

Lovely, but limited intellectually, Fee reflected sardonically. She must frequently bore him, but, as he had acknowledged, Rhodes Properties never did.

He was so full of contradictions, absorbed in his work and highly regarded as an employer, she knew, and yet simultaneously a social animal with an overt appreciation of the opposite sex, and superficial and inconsistent in his romantic attachments. But the fact that he and Charles were still friendly argued that he was at least capable of a degree of consistency in his friendships, even if he would never accept the responsibilities and curbs of marriage.

She was doing it again, Fee realised, disconcerted—looking for depths when she knew perfectly well that, as charming and physically perfect as he was, Simon was essentially a shallow man.

'Don't forget to phone on Monday,' Simon addressed Fee, ignoring Charles's challenge, and she nodded, conscious of depression settling on her, which it had tended to do ever since the Australian fiasco, as she watched him stroll away, a beautiful, truly golden man.

'Hell, it's hot. Where are my swimming-trunks, darling?' Charles gave Fee a teasing grin. 'Since Babs tells me skinny-dipping is out now that we've got you with us.'

'Find them yourself. Don't let him embarrass you, Fee, darling,' Babs adjured as he went bounding up the stairs. 'What did Simon want? He said something about a job when he arrived.'

'Yes, he said he might have a position for me at Rhodes Properties.'

'Take it,' Babs advised her promptly. 'Mercifully I don't have to work any more, but if I did Rhodes Properties would be high on my list, although I don't suppose I'd even feature on theirs. What job exactly?'

'I'm not sure. I have to ring the head of Personnel on Monday and presumably she'll decide if I qualify for whatever it is.' Fee looked at her stepsister a little uncertainly. 'It should be all right, shouldn't it, Babs? To accept if I'm offered a position, I mean? Simon did make it clear that he wasn't just being kind because I'm Charles's sister-in-law, although I gather Charles did speak to him about it. Anyway, I know he simply *isn't* a kind man.'

'No, so what are you worrying about?' Babs urged. 'I remember he used to tease you occasionally when you were a kid, but he doesn't mess around where Rhodes Properties is concerned.'

'I know. It's strange that he should have such a reputation for integrity where that side of his life is concerned, when you consider how he behaves in other areas,' Fee commented, regarding Babs with sudden curiosity. 'All those women——'

'Don't look at me like that; I wasn't one,' Babs laughed, able to read her thoughts now that she had discarded the more worldly persona she adopted for strangers. 'It was one of those lucky things. I was already falling in love with old Charlie when he introduced us, and, to my immense relief, nothing changed. To give him his due, I think Simon was equally relieved as Charles is one of the few people he genuinely likes. I know you've always loathed him—I remember you used to call him "that horrible man"—because of the teasing, not forgetting that time he lost his temper with you so abominably, but he's not as unscrupulous as he's made out to be, you know. Oh, he's a playboy of the first order but, for instance, he never gets involved with a married woman.'

'He hardly needs to when he must have a queue of single ones all lined up waiting their turn to be flavour of the month,' Fee suggested sardonically before shrugging dismissively. 'Oh, well, it doesn't matter. I do accept that where Rhodes Properties is concerned he's a different man, and if I am offered whatever job it is and whoever my immediate boss is going to be seems all right I'll probably take it.'

Babs and Charles went out a little later, urging Fee to join them, but she declined, spending a quiet evening on her own, and she was in bed by the time she heard them return soon after midnight. She had slept extra soundly for two nights running now, compensating for the weeks of fitful, shallow slumber in Australia when she had kept waking, hot with shame or often disorientated by fatigue and nightmare, thinking she was back in that hotel room in Perth, or facing a baying pack of reporters again, or listening to Vance Sheldon's demands on the phone.

But tonight, for some reason, she was restless, unable to settle, as if Simon's visit had disturbed her in some mysterious way, and she was conscious of a return of the hot resentment that had been her most consistent reaction to Simon in past years.

Nevertheless, it would be childish to let a personal feeling prevent her accepting a position at Rhodes Properties, assuming that she was offered one, and she phoned Miss Sung-Li on the Monday morning as directed.

Fee was conscious of a slight constraint about the woman's manner which suggested wariness, but her questions were strictly professional and the answers she received must have reassured her as to Fee's legitimacy as a candidate for the job because she asked her to come in with Miss Betancourt's reference for a personal interview the following morning, warning her to be prepared for a possible second interview in the afternoon.

'The position hasn't been advertised yet, but I should warn you that I have already been giving consideration to some of our established personnel since Miss Norman advised us that she was leaving us,' she cautioned Fee.

The following day, Fee dressed for the interview in accordance with both the July heat and her perception of Miss Sung-Li, in a slim linen skirt of dark cream and a cool, loose matching jacket with sleeves that stopped at the elbows, the prettily coloured bands decorating the pockets which lay flat against her hips saving the outfit from severity.

The morning was so intensely humid that she gave up the idea of catching a bus and, since she didn't want to have to deal with traffic and parking, turned down the offer of Babs's car and took a taxi, glad that the Rhodes Properties offices were on the island and not over in

Kowloon. The building was one of the most impressive this side, an elegant, graceful white spire of imposing height.

Aged about forty, Miss Sung-Li was a reserved woman and once again Fee was aware of something resembling caution in her manner, but to her relief she confined her questions to Fee's abilities and experience. Quiet and still socially shy despite her acquired poise, Fee was nevertheless confident of her professional worth and she was gratified to observe Miss Sung-Li relaxing slightly as the interview progressed.

Finally, Miss Sung-Li seemed moved to reveal something of her thoughts.

'Of course, in your previous position, you had a superior between you and the man at the top. That wouldn't be the case here, but the work is well within your capability. Nevertheless, you are very young and rather quiet. Normally I think I might have reservations on those grounds, but, as Mr Rhodes informs me that you are old acquaintances, I have to assume that you have a fair idea of what you can expect and are confident that you can cope, and know him well enough to respect that, while he demands a great deal of his employees, he demands even more of himself.'

'I didn't realise!' Fee's professional guard fell abruptly. 'Do you mean I'd be working for—for Mr Rhodes himself?'

'Didn't he explain?' Miss Sung-Li's mouth tightened as she stared at Fee, and suspicion revealed itself in her dark eyes.

'All he said was that there might be a position for me and that I should contact you.' Fee dropped her eyes, her thoughts in turmoil.

There was a silence, but finally Miss Sung-Li seemed to reach a decision.

'Yes, you would be working for Mr Rhodes himself.
Are you still interested in the position, Miss Garland?'

This time Fee was responsible for the silence. Miss
Sung-Li believed she could do the work and, as everyone
knew, Simon simply was not a kind man, so there was
no question of his charitably creating a job for her. Nor
could this be some elaborate tease; not in business hours
when time, including Miss Sung-Li's time, was money;
besides which, this slightly formidable lady would never
lend herself to any sort of hoax.

Oh, Simon probably hadn't told her what the job entailed simply because, like so many quick, clever people
whose thoughts outran speech, he had made the assumption that everyone else knew what he knew.

All she had to consider was whether she wanted the
job, and such a prestigious position, in a firm like Rhodes
Properties, wasn't one to be turned down lightly. She
might find Simon disturbing to tranquillity, but then
again, during working hours he was probably a different
man, because the shallow, social Simon Rhodes she knew
could never have prospered to the extent that he had.

'Yes.' Fee looked up. 'Yes, I am interested, Miss
Sung-Li.'

CHAPTER THREE

SILENTLY, Fee counted the seconds Miss Sung-Li spent regarding her. Five. Then a receiver was lifted from one of the phones on her desk and she seemed to speak to several people, both in English and Cantonese, before saying crisply, 'Sir? Sung-Li. I've just concluded the interview with Miss Garland. I propose to take my lunch-break late so my report will be on your desk when you return if you'll be going out? Yes...yes, sir.' She listened briefly and made a polite response before replacing the receiver and looking at Fee a little cynically. 'Mr Rhodes is on his way down. He wants you to wait for him.'

Having little choice, Fee obediently did so, answering some casual questions about Australia until Simon arrived. Even though she had been expecting him, her pulses leapt nervously when he almost erupted into the peaceful office, and she could see his instant effect on Miss Sung-Li too. Strange man, bringing people to life like this with his blazing vitality.

'Fee!' He was hyper, his mood brilliant. 'Come on, let's go and have some lunch and I can tell you about the job. I'll read your report when we get back, Miss Sung-Li, and conduct a proper interview if I think it's encouraging, and I'll get Maynah Norman to tell Fee everything she needs to know about her duties.'

By the time they were descending in a lift, Fee had managed to catch her breath.

'I didn't realise you meant I'd be working for you,' she confided gravely.

'Didn't I say?' Simon seemed surprised and then arrogantly dismissive. 'Yes, we got side-tracked, I remember, when you accused me of wanting to do Charles a favour. You should enjoy it, though. You don't mind walking, do you? There's a great place just a few blocks away.'

Hong Kong could change so quickly, and from glittering modern buildings and complicated traffic circles they passed quickly into narrow, shadowy streets, eventually coming to an entrance decorated in the traditional bright colours, beyond which five shallow stairs led down to the restaurant, obviously a favourite with the business community as the men and women lunching there were all immaculately attired for the office. Simon was known, greeted by name and deferentially led to one of the best tables, and Fee couldn't help a feeling of general pleasure which she expressed with a contented sigh.

'It's just nice to be back and get the feel of Hong Kong again,' she explained in response to Simon's amusedly questioning glance.

'You were in Sydney, weren't you? I should have looked you up the couple of times I've been there. Where were you living?' Simon asked.

'We had a flat in Manly for the first two years, and after that I shared a house with some Aussie girls at Dee Why, just above the beach,' Fee vouchsafed, thinking how she would miss it and the local restaurants they had patronised at weekends.

'What happened to the two girls who went with you?'

'One is backpacking in Europe with a boyfriend, the other is married. She has just had her second baby,' Fee added tenderly and felt an irrational sense of outrage mixed with disappointment when Simon grimaced. 'Don't you like children?'

'Don't know much about them.' The subject plainly bored him and he turned his attention to the wine list that had just been handed to him, courteously seeking her approval of his choice. 'I just hope you won't toss it over me this time.'

Fee's eyes darkened. 'These days the responsibility lies with you.'

'In other words, I mustn't provoke you?' His glance sparkled with enjoyment, holding hers for a moment, then straying to an extremely pretty Chinese girl at a nearby table and finally returning to Fee.

She laughed, unable to help herself. 'She's beautiful, isn't she?'

'Lovely. You're an unusual one, Fee.' Simon sounded mildly intrigued. 'Generous. Most women I know get furiously uptight if the man they're with so much as glances at another woman, even if he means nothing to them personally. They start tearing the other woman to shreds and, in my experience, the more beautiful a woman is, the bitchier she'll be about other beauties.'

'I suppose it's understandable,' Fee suggested compassionately. 'So much is made of beauty that they start believing it's all they've got without being able to forget that it doesn't last, so they become desperately insecure. It doesn't apply in my case, though, because I'm not beautiful.'

'No.' He brought the word out slowly, studying her face thoughtfully, bright, clever eyes lingering on the curve of her nose, the soft flush of her mouth and the way her cheekbones swept downwards from just beneath the delicate hollows at her temples. 'No, you aren't exactly.'

That could just be why he had decided it might suit him to have her working for him, Fee reflected wryly. He was intelligent enough to recognise his own weaknesses and, since he did take Rhodes Properties seriously, he probably didn't like being distracted during working hours.

On leaving Australia, she had promised herself that she would be scrupulously careful in her choice of boss in future, and she had anticipated a long search, but it seemed as if she might have been lucky, because if she got the Rhodes Properties job she wouldn't need to be afraid of Simon's turning out to be like Vance Sheldon, however badly he might behave with the legions of beautiful women who did attract him.

She felt confident that she could do the job Simon outlined over lunch and she was even optimistic that he might prove to be less disconcerting as a boss than he was as an acquaintance.

However, as they walked back to Rhodes Properties, he seemed inclined to revert to personal topics.

'How are things at home? What have you been doing with yourself?'

'Oh, nothing much.'

'Not trying to take up where you and Bates left off?' Simon prompted smoothly. 'I can imagine that the contrast of his youth might appeal to you after that old man you were involved with in Australia.'

'As you say, that old man,' Fee emphasised, incensed by his lack of intuition. 'Doesn't that even suggest that you might be wrong about the nature of my "involvement" with him?'

'What's wrong? Did he fail to satisfy you?' he derided lightly and laughed at her furious expression. 'But then again, Bates is too young for you, not much more than a boy. What you really need in a relationship is a man——'

'If ever I find myself in need of advice about relationships, I'll apply to someone with a more successful record than yours, thanks, Simon,' she cut in caustically, inwardly disconcerted by the personal turn the conversation had taken.

'I don't consider any of my relationships to have been failures,' Simon returned easily, observing her with amused eyes.

Fee laughed incredulously. 'They haven't exactly lasted, have they? You've never married, for instance.'

'Marriage is scarcely a proof of success,' he drawled mockingly. 'In fact, most marriages look like failures to me, even when the people concerned make an effort to keep up appearances. Have you ever seen one that works?'

'What about Babs and Charles?' Fee demanded rebelliously.

'They're probably on their best behaviour when other people are around,' Simon retorted.

'Your cynicism really is total and irremediable, isn't it?' she taunted.

'I call it realism,' he returned with a laugh. 'No, Fee, I've never regarded myself as a cynic.'

'You don't believe in love,' she reminded him acidly.

'But I do,' he contradicted her, clearly enjoying himself. 'But in love ephemeral, not love eternal, and undoing a marriage can be a complicated business. Not that I wouldn't like to believe in the sort of thing you obviously believe Charles and Babs have got. I think I'd quite like to be loved in some unreserved, wholly committed way, not in spite of all my faults, but with them, because they're accepted as part of me.'

'You ask a lot,' Fee commented drily, thinking of his particular faults.

'Yes, I suppose I do,' he conceded insouciantly. 'Only I don't really, because, as I say, I don't believe in that sort of thing, I don't need it. How can anyone need something that doesn't exist?'

He was so confident, so utterly free of doubts about the cynical code that dictated his lifestyle, that Fee was piqued.

'I suppose all your parents' marriages have put you off?' she guessed flippantly.

Simon flung her a derisive look. 'Quit the amateur psychology, sweetheart. It's hardly original, either, if you're running away with the idea that I'm influenced by the turbulent lives my parents and their various partners led. No one influences me. Only the weak let others shape their thinking.'

'But we're all affected by the people we come into contact with because none of us can exist entirely in isolation,' Fee responded sharply. 'It's only weakness if we're influenced against our will, and its very obvious that the life you lead isn't against yours. You've chosen it, it suits you.'

But she thought his parents' notoriously frequent marriages and divorces probably had affected him, even if he either didn't believe it or wouldn't admit it.

A mocking glint was evident in Simon's eyes. 'I want an assistant, Fee, not a shrink or a philosopher.'

'It was you who dragged the conversation down to a personal level first,' she reminded him tartly, 'going on about Warren and Mr Sheldon.'

Unexpectedly, he laughed. 'Or is it just that you enjoy arguing with me? Still making up for the days when you were too shy to answer back?'

It could well be that, she reflected sardonically. Certainly, something about Simon seemed to challenge her, making her unusually contrary-minded, gripped by a need to contradict and question everything he said, but perhaps she ought to start trying to conquer the impulse if she wanted the job he was offering her.

But not yet!

'You're not my boss yet,' she mentioned sweetly, and he laughed again.

'Oh, I won't expect doormat docility even when I am.'

They had reached Rhodes Properties and Simon told her to come up to the floor on which he had his suite of offices. In the outer room he introduced her to Maynah Norman, a slim, attractive platinum-blonde in her mid-twenties.

'Maynah can give you some idea of what the job entails while I go through Miss Sung-Li's assessment. Then I'll probably have a few questions of my own to ask you,' he warned her and disappeared into his own office.

'Unfortunately I won't be around to ease you into the job,' Maynah cautioned Fee after giving her an outline of her duties and the methods Simon insisted on as well as answering her questions. 'I've told Simon and Personnel that I want to leave as soon as they decide on my replacement, but you shouldn't find it too daunting, especially as I gather you've known Simon for some years.'

'Since I was a teenager,' Fee admitted.

'So you must be used to him. Immune too, probably. Lucky you,' Maynah added fervently, smiling wryly as Fee's eyes widened. 'Oh, you must know that most of us aren't. That's why I'm leaving. He has never been interested in me, of course; he doesn't like women with brains, only silly, giggling little socialites. But for a long time I accepted it, if only I could be near him. I'd never have believed I could have so little pride, living for the sight of him, knowing I didn't have a chance. But lately... I suppose it's reviving pride. I'm not prepared to go on doing that to myself, living on dreams. Naturally, he thinks I should stay and sweat it out.'

The conclusion was tinged with bitterness and Fee felt both compassion and embarrassment as she saw that tears were standing in Maynah's sapphire eyes.

'He knows...?' Sensitively, she abandoned the question, sudden anger turning her own eyes almost black as she recalled Simon's comments about the lack of reason behind Mynah's resignation.

'Oh, he knows,' Maynah confirmed, her lips trembling. 'But he can't see my point—he can't put himself in my place. He thinks I'll simply fall in love with someone else one of these fine days and the problem will have solved itself. Maybe I am capable of loving someone else, maybe I'm not, but I'm never going to find out for sure while I'm still seeing him every day, because I just don't see other men at the moment. Simon has blinded me, if you like. If you've known him so long, I suppose he thinks it's an advantage, that he won't have to put up with the same sort of inconvenience all over again, because if you haven't been as stupid as I have before now then you're unlikely to be at this late stage either.'

It could be true, Fee reflected. She still felt oddly angry, though, mostly on Mynah's behalf, although Simon's callous attitude shouldn't have surprised her.

The anger was still evident when she was summoned to his office.

'Ah, Fee.' Simon was seated behind a large desk, looking at a slim folder of papers, but he rose as she entered. 'I see from this Miss Betancourt's report that you did in fact resign from the job in Australia. The desperately determined way you were talking about everlasting love earlier had me wondering if the stories about Sheldon firing you might be true after all and you were still yearning for him, but obviously you were the one who tired of the relationship first and were responsible for that very public break-up. I suppose he couldn't accept it and you felt compelled to leave rather than sit it out until he got over you.'

'The way Mynah is supposed to get over you?' Fee hadn't intended to say that, but the angry words came tumbling out before she could stop them and, hearing herself, she paused to draw a controlling breath, dropping her bag on to one of the chairs facing the desk. 'She says you know why she's leaving.'

'Yes, I know,' Simon agreed flatly. 'It's her decision, but I don't see why she couldn't have toughed it out, especially when I've tactfully ignored the whole thing up until now, for both our sakes. She'd have got over me eventually. Love——'

'—doesn't last,' Fee got in swiftly in a softly taunting chant, eyes sparkling with furious derision because there it was again, the emphasis she found so abrasive to her own beliefs concerning love.

He just laughed appreciatively. 'You're really getting to know me, aren't you? But why are you so angry?'

'All my life I've kept falling over women in floods of tears because of you—Ismay Compton for instance, and——'

'Now that has to be an exaggeration,' Simon drawled, still sounding amused. 'You haven't known me all your life.'

'Mercifully,' Fee snapped.

'So what exactly is the matter?' He seemed utterly unperturbed.

It made her pause, because she didn't really know. His dismissal of Maynah's feelings was callous, yes, but she shouldn't be reacting quite so strongly, especially when her sensitive imagination forced her to sympathise to a certain degree. He must get so tired of women falling in love with him.

'Nothing is the matter,' she finally said bitingly, eyes blazing. 'In fact, everything is perfect, and if you're going to offer me this job it will suit me fine—and suit you even better, obviously. That's why you actually bothered even considering me when Charles came hinting to you, isn't it? Because you know I'm not one of your

adorers so you'll be safe from having to feel embarrassed or guilty—not that you've ever cared about any
of the poor idiots before, but perhaps you're tired of
being adored, because everything bores you eventually,
doesn't it?'

Fee could hear herself going on and on, and she was
disconcerted again. It really would suit her perfectly because she had wanted a boss she could rely on not to
start seeing her as Vance Sheldon had—so why was she
so incensed?

'Where in the world have you got hold of all these
strange ideas—both about me and about yourself?'
Simon gestured expressively, still completely unaffected
by her fury. 'Fee, darling, all I require of my assistant
is efficiency—which Maynah provided. The rest was irrelevant, although in your case adoration would be a
bonus and I'd be delighted.'

Fee gasped and she was staring at him, unable to believe what she was hearing, but finally it registered.

'You must have the most incredible ego!' she raged
scornfully. 'What sort of satisfaction does that give you,
having even those women who don't interest or attract
you falling in love with you—worshipping you?'

'Hell, if you think I suffer from that sort of vanity,
you can't know me so well after all. Why shouldn't you
interest and attract me, please tell me?' Simon invited
her smoothly, following it with a blazing smile. 'In fact,
Fee, you could quite easily turn out to be the next woman
in my life. Would you enjoy that? I think I would.'

Heat flooded Fee's face. 'I cannot imagine a fate more
appalling. Very funny, Simon. I thought you were supposed to be responsible where Rhodes Properties is concerned, however much you fool around away from work.'

His smile vanished as he heard the resentful note. 'Oh,
I agree, this is hardly the occasion and it's something
we'd do better to pursue at our leisure, but, since the

subject has arisen, let's not be too strict with ourselves. The world isn't going to end if we occasionally happen to discuss personal matters in between business.'

'There's nothing personal to discuss,' she flared, feeling rather desperate suddenly.

'Aren't you over-reacting?' Simon enquired coolly. 'I merely commented to the effect that you could well turn out to be the next woman in my life, darling.'

Was that what Vance Sheldon had started out thinking? But Fee still couldn't quite bring herself to believe that Simon was serious. He had to be teasing her.

'Just how gullible do you think I am, Simon?' she demanded tautly.

Simon frowned. 'Gullible in what way?'

'This is a joke, isn't it?' Fee condemned, striving to quell the emotional agitation suddenly afflicting her. 'I remember how you used to tease me sometimes...'

'When you were a kid, which you're not now. Oh, I know you're not my usual type—small and either sassy or dumb—but I imagine you see what I see when you look at yourself in a mirror. It's not strictly beauty, but there's a certain tender sophistication, and all that sensual grace...something I never visualised your acquiring even if you lost the clumsiness. But, in view of the way you're reacting to a casual comment, I've an idea that there are other things from the past, some excess emotional baggage, that you have yet to discard,' he observed thoughtfully, a speculative gleam in the brilliant blue eyes. 'You were a child then, and I treated you as such, but you've come home a lovely and desirable young woman with a welcome amount of experience behind you, obviously, and I for one am delighted, even if no one else can see it.'

'If that's true——' Fee was convinced that she was probably making a fool of herself by even considering the possibility that it might be '—it's because you're bored, isn't it? You've always got any woman you've ever wanted, quite easily, but you know I don't like you and that I'll never——'

'Oh, not that old cliché about being a challenge to me,' Simon interrupted derisively, laughter lurking in his eyes now. 'I'm not one of those men who claims to enjoy that sort of challenge. I've never really believed them anyway. I think I'd find it far too damaging to my pride to have to pursue a woman who kept on resisting and rejecting me, and only a total animal could take any satisfaction from an unwilling woman if his patience ran out.'

'Then you won't be...pursuing me, will you?' Fee prompted caustically, still utterly sceptical.

'Meaning you'll be resisting me?' Frustratingly, Simon didn't give her a direct answer, and Fee grew very still as he moved out from behind the desk. 'We'll see, won't we? It's quite possible that once you accept that we have a new relationship these days, that I no longer regard you as a child and won't treat you like one, you may find that you don't want to resist me after all.'

His arrogance was outrageous, and Fee gave him a scalding smile, her eyes dark with denial.

'Because no one else ever does? I could never be interested in someone like you, Simon,' she asserted passionately. 'I don't even like you, and, if I did, with all the women you've been involved with, all the women I've seen crying over you——'

'They come into the relationships with their eyes wide open, so I don't know why they depart crying.' The dismissal was ruthless.

'Maynah Norman wasn't *in* any sort of personal relationship with you.' Fee's voice shook with rage.

'Then I'm not responsible for whatever she feels, because I haven't encouraged her.' Simon's voice was hard, without a trace of either compassion or compunction, and Fee winced for Maynah and however many others there were like her. 'But I think I could end up encouraging you, Fee.'

His voice had dropped now, assuming a warmly caressing note, and apprehension made her pulses leap as she realised how close to her he was suddenly.

'You just don't care, do you?' she accused him tempestuously, gripped by a terrible tension now. 'You may love women, but you don't respect them. All they're good for is entertaining you—pleasing you until you get tired of them. You amuse yourself at the expense of their feelings, and now you think you've found a new way of amusing yourself, with me, by dragging me into this pointless argument, but I'm not playing. This is supposed to be an interview, remember?'

'In fact, an interview is superfluous since I know you, know the person you are, while Miss Sung-Li's assessment and the Betancourt reference have told me all I need to know about your abilities and experience. But we'll keep it formal for now—Miss Sung-Li will be contacting you and offering you the position—because once you're officially hired as my assistant we'll have to confine this sort of thing to after-hours.'

Simon's hands had come to rest lightly on her shoulders, and Fee was suddenly trembling violently as they now slid confidently down to her back. Otherwise, she found herself unexpectedly incapable of movement. His hands were gently massaging as if he sought to ease her tension, his arms were strong, and she was possessed by a treacherous urge to lean, to let him support and soothe her and take away all the terrible, humiliating things that had happened to her in recent weeks and keep her safe.

But no woman who yielded to Simon Rhodes was ever safe for long. He broke hearts...

Her lips shook beneath the light touch of his mouth, and her eyes fluttered closed—just for a moment, she promised herself, to see what it was like. This was what he did to other women, the women who loved him...

Simon's lips were warm, lazily exploratory, nudging and encouraging, and Fee couldn't stop a sigh that sounded suspiciously like one of surrender as her hands moved of their own accord to his upper arms and clung, discovering the reassuring strength and solidity of the taut muscles beneath the fine expensive fabric of his jacket.

He accepted the involuntary invitation confidently, deepening the kiss with a sure sensuality that altered and intensified the nature of her trembling as a sweetly piercing thrill of sensation manifested itself in the core of her being. Her mouth felt all tingling and sparkling, responding tentatively now to the warmly erotic play of his, and Simon had drawn her closer, making her body aware of the power of his.

'You see, Fee,' he murmured against her lips as he ended the kiss, 'you've only come back to Hong Kong. You haven't gone back in time. You're still the woman that man in Australia found so irresistible. Others as well, I imagine. And a woman I too find desirable.'

Fee had stiffened at the mention of Australia.

'Let me go,' she demanded in a stifled voice and he did, glancing at his watch and laughing softly.

'That was interesting... and very promising,' he commented with offensive nonchalance. 'I'm encouraged to pursue it, but unfortunately I've got a meeting in five or ten minutes. Miss Sung-Li will be in touch with you.'

'I'm not sure I want the job after all,' Fee began tempestuously, snatching up her bag.

'Why not?' Simon enquired silkily, a dangerous glint in his eyes. 'What's changed? All right, you've just discovered that you're capable of responding to me, but you don't seem to have had any objection to mixing business and pleasure in the past.'

'Pleasure?' Fee was scathing. 'Your arrogance is amazing, but that's why Miss Sung-Li *can* contact me if that's the way it's done at Rhodes—because I'd dearly love to prove to you that you're not as irresistible as you think you are.'

'When can you start?' There was a wicked charm to Simon's insouciant smile. 'Maynah wants out as soon as possible——'

'I haven't said I'm definitely accepting,' she cautioned him sharply. 'I said Miss Sung-Li could contact me, and I will consider what she has to say very carefully, with reference to both my future interests *and* the things you've just been saying to me, because the one thing I don't need in my life is a repeat of what happened in Australia... Although I suppose I should see the funny side. Apparently I have a peculiar attraction for older men! First there was Mr Sheldon, and now there's you. Thank you for seeing me.'

Simon's mouth had tightened and as she saw his eyes begin to blaze Fee gave him a taunting little smile before turning and leaving, recognising the signs and quite unable to face his temper. Once in a lifetime had been too often, never to be forgotten.

Horrible, mocking, promiscuous man! But, unlike Vance Sheldon, at least Simon had been open about his intentions—assuming he had any and hadn't just been flirting, amusing himself by testing her reaction to him, or trying to find out just how much she really had grown up during the years she had been away.

When she got outside the building, she found that clouds had come up to cover the sky although the sun still blazed through them, dulled to silver and turning the city into a sauna.

It *might* be all right to accept the job. She knew Simon, after all...

But just in case she decided against it and had to spend weeks looking for another, she had better economise by catching a bus home, if only she could remember the number for the buses that went out to Repulse Bay and then find a stop on that route, because the only terminus she recalled was quite a distance away.

She had to ask twice and was misdirected once, but at last she was seated on the correct bus and able to give her attention to a number of questions. The rain was lancing down by the time she reached Repulse Bay, and she had no umbrella with her, but she hardly noticed, still preoccupied.

She thought she was justified in assuming that she would always know where she stood with Simon—he wouldn't hide his strictly dishonourable intentions the way Vance Sheldon had done—but all the same, she wasn't going to rush into a decision.

There was her reaction to him to be considered, for one thing. She hadn't liked that, the way she had forgotten everything in his arms, and the memory made her flush.

Babs met her at the door when she reached the house.

'Baby, you're soaked. But how did it go?'

'I'm not sure. I'd be working for Simon himself, so I think I need to consider everything involved very carefully.'

But her natural reticence stopped her elaborating, and Babs seemed to assume that her doubts stemmed from her old dislike of Simon, leaving her to go upstairs and shower.

The rain continued into the evening, so later, dressed in jeans and a soft, loose T-shirt, Fee sat with Babs and Charles at the bar in one corner of the large covered patio, Charles leaping up when they heard the front doorbell ring. A few minutes later, he brought the caller out to the patio.

'Here's Simon,' he announced unnecessarily as Fee tensed, sensing instinctively that his presence concerned her.

'I hope this isn't inconvenient, but Fee called me ancient and walked out on me before I'd said all I had to, so I thought I'd take a chance on finding her here,' he told the others, flicking Fee an idly mocking glance.

Charles was laughing. 'Making the most of your opportunities before he becomes your boss and you have to start being respectful, little one?'

'I haven't accepted the job yet,' Fee stated firmly, defiance sparkling in her eyes as they met Simon's. 'In fact, I haven't even had a formal offer yet.'

'You will,' Simon promised. 'But I'm not here about that. I've talked to someone in our residential division and brought you a list of places you might like to view as you've said you'd be looking for somewhere. I imagine you're not interested in the central high-rise districts, so these are small blocks, all here on the island and some not that far from here. Of course, once you're working for us, you'll qualify for our subsidised home-owning scheme, but I'd recommend that you rent to begin with and not rush into anything.'

He was so confident that she would accept the job that Fee was incensed, but she had to turn her attention to Babs who was objecting agitatedly.

'Oh, you don't want to move out, Fee, and how will you cope? You've never lived alone before, even in Australia.'

'Then don't you think it's time I did?' Fee prompted gently. 'But I was thinking of looking for something around Repulse Bay, so I won't be far away, Babs. Only I don't need Simon's——'

There were phones all over the house and even one out here on the bar counter, and she stopped, jumping as it rang, nervous of the things since Australia. Babs answered it, giving the Sandilands name and number.

'No... Yes, I'll call her.' She held the receiver out to Fee. 'For you, Fee.'

Feel slid off her stool a little awkwardly and took the receiver apprehensively. She was being silly. This was Hong Kong and it would be Warren or another of her old friends, since she didn't suppose she would be hearing from Miss Sung-Li until the morning.

'Fee,' she identified herself quietly and drew a sharp breath as she recognised the distinctive characteristics of an international call, that slight hum and the un-naturally long pause.

'Now look, I've had enough of this nonsense of yours. You had no right to pull out like that. I want you back here...'

Fee had gone pale, her eyes closing, and when she opened them again they looked like twin bruises against the pallor of her face. How had he found her here?

The angry demands continued, burning into her ear as she tried to focus on something—anything—while she wondered desperately how she could stop him once and for all. She was so tired of hearing that voice, so tired of being reminded!

Simon's tanned face swam before her; then her vision cleared and she saw the dawning realisation in his eyes.

'Put it down, Fee. *Put it down*,' he repeated urgently, but she was paralysed, the receiver seemingly glued into her hand as she stared at him.

He came to her then, prising the receiver out of her convulsive grip, his other hand dropping to her shoulder and pushing her gently away so that she could no longer hear any actual words although that bullying voice still went on and on.

Simon hesitated only a second before putting the receiver to his own ear, his fingers tightening over Fee's shoulder as he did so. She saw his mouth compress, rage blazing in his eyes, but he only listened a moment or two before speaking.

'Sheldon, I presume? My name is Rhodes. Miss Garland has already answered you very clearly by leaving Australia, I think, so this is pointless and constitutes harassment. That's the only warning you'll get.'

Then he put the receiver down.

Fee swayed, held by a despairing weariness as she realised that as long as Vance Sheldon refused to accept defeat she wasn't going to be allowed to forget what had happened.

'She's going to faint,' she heard Babs warning above Charles's colourful cursing, and she was dimly conscious of Simon supporting her as she sagged, and telling Babs to pull up one of the low seats from the other side of the patio.

'No, I'm not,' she insisted furiously, recovering slightly.

But Simon and Babs were pushing her down on to the seat, Babs clutching at her.

'She has to put her head between her knees, I think.' Babs sounded as panicky as she had when they were little and some disaster had befallen one or other of them during one of Angela's absences and she would be paging frantically through the emergency first-aid book they had used some of their intermittent pocket-money to order from a local newspaper. 'It's all my fault! What did that man want? I should never have let her go to Australia. She's only a baby!'

'Stop being ridiculous, Barbara,' Simon snapped. 'And stop strangling her. Then she might be all right.'

'I am.' Fee raised her head, trying hard to pretend as she always had done, for Babs's sake. 'Sorry, I just thought...I thought I'd be safe here.'

'You are,' Simon and Babs spoke in unison and Simon added, 'Quite safe, Fee. Charles? What was she drinking?'

'Coke.'

'Brandy,' Simon ordered succinctly.

'I'll spill it over you,' Fee gasped, striving to produce a laugh. 'I don't need it. Dammit, Simon—all of you—leave me alone!'

But, to her shame, she was aware of tears filling her eyes and she ducked her head hastily so that they wouldn't see, but it was too late. Typically, Babs immediately shared her distress, while Charles was vowing to hunt Vance Sheldon down and wring his neck. Then, to her relief, Simon took charge.

CHAPTER FOUR

'GO AWAY, Simon. She won't want to see you now. Don't you realise how upset she is after that phone call? Fee is very sensitive.'

Guarding the door to the bedroom, Babs sounded more drunk than Fee felt, which seemed all wrong because Babs was accustomed to sipping a fair quantity of spirits in the evenings, whereas Fee seldom drank anything stronger than wine. The fact that they were both at least tipsy now could be blamed on Simon, as he had sent them upstairs with a whole bottle of brandy.

Guilt gnawed at Fee as she identified the mood Babs was in. She had experienced it so often in the past—the protectiveness that made her love Babs all the more but which simultaneously exasperated.

'She's *over*-sensitive, and you make her that way,' she heard Simon retort. 'She wouldn't be nearly so upset if you hadn't put on such a melodramatic performance of your own. We're talking about a woman who has been around and is accustomed to taking care of herself, remember, but if you're stupid enough to try to cosset her it's natural that she's going to give in and let you—let herself be weak.'

His perspicacity was alarming to Fee, but she raised her voice, calling to Babs with reluctant honesty, 'He's right, Babs. I'm twenty-two. I have to fight my own battles even if I lose them. Let him in.'

There was a brief silence before Simon entered her bedroom. He had still been in the suit he had worn earlier in the day when he arrived, but he had discarded both jacket and tie by now.

'Battles, Fee?' he challenged in a softly mocking tone, eyes gleaming with enjoyment. 'Are we going to fight, then?'

'Probably,' Fee snapped, rising from the edge of the bed on which she had been sitting. 'I suppose you're expecting me to thank you for dealing with that phone call, but I could have handled it myself quite well. You've got a nerve, you know, talking to Babs like that, criticising the way she treats me when you've just been guilty of the same sort of thing, taking the phone away from me, sending me upstairs with a bottle of brandy——'

Simon held up a pacifying hand.

'You went, didn't you? All right, all right, calm down,' he advised her sardonically. 'Your reaction caused me to leap to the erroneous conclusion that you were the victim of an obscene call, something not even the toughest of women finds easy to shrug off, but obviously you were just treating us to a glimpse of the old Fee—naturally enough, I suppose, because no one's personality ever changes completely—and the call was in fact a plea, if somewhat aggressive. The guy wants you back.'

'In my job,' Fee asserted tautly, sitting down again because the brandy seemed to have impaired her legs' ability to support her. 'He never had me in any other way.'

'No, clearly your heart wasn't involved there since you've told me love didn't come into it. What was it, then, sex or his ability to give you a good time materially and socially?' Instead of taking the chair next to the window or the dressing-table stool, Simon sat down beside her, turning towards her in order to see her face, which was still pale, before continuing musingly, 'No, not the latter because you're not that sort of person.

You've never been a raver. Sex, then. Well, he's supposed to be a personable man if somewhat long in the tooth... But what the hell did you do to him? He must be crazy about you if he's willing to make a fool of himself like that, begging you to come back. Absolutely smitten!'

Fee gave him a quick resentful look and averted her face.

'No, he just doesn't like being thwarted,' she corrected, a trace of bitterness seeping through her artificial composure.

'Is that a streak of sadism manifesting itself there, or are you only just discovering your power as a woman now? In which case I imagine you can't resist experimenting with it, testing its range and capacity so to speak.' Simon was idly taunting, holding her eyes and smiling as he observed her angry reaction. 'No, I don't think you're really a cruel person. It's obvious you have some grievance against the man, but why did you choose to punish him so publicly? Was he refusing to leave his wife for you or something? But from the way he was carrying on tonight, demanding your return like that, you can hardly see yourself as a woman scorned, darling.'

The cynical assumptions he was making about her raised her anger to the level of defiant rage.

'You're not in a position to know what you're talking about,' she derided blisteringly. 'But it's none of your business anyway, and I'm not going to pander to your sense of your own importance by telling you what really happened. You'd never understand if I did, as it is.'

As she said it, it occurred to her somewhat disconcertingly that she didn't actually want him to understand, because if he did he would also understand the pathetically short distance she had travelled from the gauche teenager he had once been able to reduce to a blushing, stammering emotional mess of resentment and embarrassment. Inwardly she felt terrifyingly like that girl still, but somehow it had become vitally important that she shouldn't reveal any vulnerability to Simon Rhodes.

'I'm not sure I want to, although I can guess quite easily,' he claimed in a confident murmur, utterly unperturbed by her furious rejection. 'These old men often get possessive, sometimes obsessively so, once they break out and find themselves a sweet young thing. If it was the first time he'd strayed, it would make it even worse; he'd be frantic about the loss of his trophy... I think you're realising that, aren't you? But boys like Bates aren't the answer for someone like you either.'

'I'm not looking for answers—by which I suppose you really mean lovers,' Fee guessed, treating him to a deliberate, sharp-sweet smile. 'I suppose this preoccupation with age is because I implied you were old earlier today. In fact, I just wanted to annoy you.'

'That did occur to me. No, I'm not in my dotage yet. On the contrary, I consider myself to be the perfect age,' he informed her complacently.

'For what?' she retorted, and wished she hadn't when the gleam in his eyes grew more pronounced.

'For you?' Simon suggested.

'You may think so.' Her tone was stinging. 'You would! But I don't.'

'You know I'm right really.' Infuriatingly, the arrogance came accompanied by such charm of voice and warmth of smile that Fee felt a precariously yielding sensation somewhere within her. 'That's why you're making such a major production of denying it. For all your experience, I think you're still essentially a gentle creature. What you need is a man's strength, not the weakness I suspect is integral to a youth like Bates.'

'A man's strength—to lean on?' Fee was scathing, her eyes sparkling with contempt.

'When necessary, when you want to,' Simon agreed easily. 'But also the strength that allows you to be yourself as opposed to the tyranny that oppresses, which is what Sheldon seems to have been trying to do to you.'

'Your strength, of course?'

Belatedly she wondered if it was wise to be challenging him so directly, but as always he seemed to be calling to her fighting spirit and she couldn't stop herself answering the summons.

'Quite possibly. Why not?' he prompted with lazy humour.

'And what about Loren Kincaid?'

'I'm dealing with her...subtly,' he added softly.

'Deviously,' Fee guessed scornfully.

He shrugged, undisturbed. 'Since the direct way I dealt with Ismay Compton a few years ago put you in such a paddy, I thought you might look more favourably on a fine Italian hand this time around.'

'The brutal way,' Fee corrected him with a faint inward shiver at the thought of the intellectual rings this clever man could run round everyone if ever he seriously chose to go in for real deviousness.

'Either way, don't let it bother you.' Simon was insouciantly dismissive. 'It's my responsibility, not yours.'

He really was outrageous. Fee shook her head. Of course it would bother her. She had liked Loren——

Oh, God, she was actually starting to believe in all this nonsense of his.

She regarded Simon warily and he looked back at her, the gathering warmth in his eyes bringing a slow flush to her face which deepened as he gave her an indolent yet openly seductive smile.

'I'm not sure I believe any of this,' she commented slowly, achieving a coolly amused little smile.

Simon laughed softly. He was still turned towards her and he lifted a hand to touch her face lightly, a long finger tracing the curve of her cheek.

'You must know just how desirable you are, sweetheart,' he was drawling, giving her another lazy smile as his arm slid round her shoulders. 'And you haven't got any complicated hang-ups about desire, have you? In fact, I've an idea you're a very simple, giving person, and that you'll prove to be incredibly generous.'

'Generous? To you, Simon?' she managed sceptically, but at the same time there was a little catch in her voice as she found herself drawn fully into the curve of his arm, the hand on her shoulder sliding down over her upper arm while she felt the fingers of his other hand nudge gently from below at the delicate line of her jaw.

'Again, why not?' Simon murmured confidently, his breath stirring the dark curls that tumbled over her brow. 'In time, Fee, in time.'

A tiny sigh escaped her as he cradled her body close against his. It was so tempting to surrender to the shelter his embrace seemed to offer. Not that she was attracted to him, of course, but the world had seemed such an abrasive place just lately and Simon was so sure and strong and warm, a confident man whom nothing could seriously trouble, capable of dealing with any situation.

The longing was causing a tight, hurting sensation in her breast. Her eyes closed, long lashes casting shadows over her pale cheeks, and she found her parted lips touching the firmness of Simon's.

'It's all right,' he reassured her easily as she drew back in embarrassment. 'Don't stop there... You taste of brandy.'

Not surprisingly, Fee reflected, wondering if she was seriously drunk as she opened her eyes again to focus on the sensual, masculine curve of the mouth hers had sought so involuntarily.

'Simon, I don't think . . .'

'No, don't think for a minute or two,' he urged, sounding amused.

This time it was his lips that found hers and Fee shivered, oddly *distraite* for a moment before accepting the kiss and—oh, admittedly!—responding to it. His mouth was so warm; it moved on hers and in it with such tender eroticism, and she drew him further in, helplessly awash with sensation. One hand lay curled against his chest and she could feel the healthy, powerful beat of his heart beneath her fingers.

'Nice?' Simon questioned her languidly, letting his hand drop to rest lightly over one slight, cotton-covered breast.

A shuddery sigh escaped Fee as her mouth returned to his. This time his kiss was deeper, more masterful and almost possessive, and Fee felt her trembling body growing hot and restless. Long fingers stirred gently against her breast, setting up tremors of desire that went thrilling through her entire being.

'Oh, very nice,' Simon confirmed teasingly, his hand dropping confidently to her lap, turning the tremors to an ongoing quake.

Fee had lifted her hand to the powerful golden column of his throat, fingers exploring wonderingly. He was a golden man altogether, and she had never touched anyone so beautiful before.

'I hardly think nice is the word.' Her voice had a break in it, making her sound languidly sensual, on the verge of surrender.

Oh, God, what was she doing and saying? No wonder Simon was looking at her with such idle satisfaction. Quite unmistakable, it lit his eyes and curved his mouth.

'No, just nice for now,' he insisted softly. 'The rest comes later and I promise you it will be worthy of all the superlatives we can think of.'

'You're seducing me while I'm drunk,' Fee complained, finally finding the strength of will to lower her hand and remove his from its intimate resting place.

'No, not seducing you, not tonight. Just tempting you with a taste of delight to come,' he corrected her wickedly, finally freeing her. 'And never here, dear Fee. Not in this house, with your stepsister liable to come rushing in to rescue her darling from my evil clutches. The sooner you move into a place of your own, the better. I've left that list of apartments to view downstairs, incidentally.'

Fee stared at him, not yet fully liberated from the spell he had woven about her, the sweet, enveloping golden magic of desire.

Then, with an effort, she freed herself.

'Just stop trying to organise my life for me, Simon,' she instructed him tightly.

'Don't be so touchy.' He stood up, smiling down at her. 'Helping someone out when it's no trouble is a natural part of ordinary, normal social commerce, not an attempt to take over, and you've said you need somewhere of your own... Unless you'd like to move into my place if and when we start a proper affair? I'm still in that house on the Peak and I think you ought to be happy there.'

His tone had grown wickedly suggestive again and Fee couldn't control a blush, just praying that he would mistake it for the flush of anger.

'You're assuming a lot, aren't you? What makes you think I'd be happy to have an affair with you in the first place?'

Fully recovered now and hating herself for whatever it was that had made her so weak and willing in his arms, Fee too was on her feet.

'The way you've just been kissing me, for one thing,' Simon returned incorrigibly.

'And what about Loren Kincaid?' she demanded once more, infuriated by his flippancy. 'Does she move out before or after I've moved in?'

'I haven't had her living there. She has a nice place of her own, and I've generally preferred to make separate establishments the rule; it makes splitting up easier and parting less painful when there's no packing to be done; but I'd be prepared to make a rare exception in your case.'

'You are unbelievable,' Fee blazed at him, the colour in her cheeks no longer anything to do with embarrassment. 'Get this, Simon, there's no way I want to be part of your complicated love life, now or ever. I don't know how you do it without giving yourself an ulcer. It's incredible! You're *juggling* with Loren and me—as you seem to think!'

'Wrong, darling. Loren is about to become part of my past.' Simon was remorseless and compassion for Loren wrenched at Fee's heart.

'And next it will be my turn? No, thanks, Simon, I don't even like you, but even if I did, I don't hate myself that much,' she averred stormily. 'I've seen what you do to women, I've seen it all before. I've been watching it since I was a child. They all end up crying.'

'But not you.' Simon was completely unmoved and still devastatingly sure of himself and of her. 'You know what I'm like, better than most, just because you have been watching me for so long, as you say, so you won't have any illusions to be shattered, and nor will you make the mistake of thinking you can change me.'

Fee was enraged, but somehow she managed to control herself, dropping her voice to a sweetly taunting note. 'But they nearly all go into the affairs like that, knowing there's a time limit, don't they, Simon? And still it ends in tears. I said no, thanks! You break hearts.'

'People let their hearts be broken,' he contradicted her mildly. 'But the whole business is largely imaginary, born of a pandemic tendency to dramatise the end of a relationship. I've never understood it personally, when endings are as natural as beginnings, and inevitable— because love and attraction are natural things and every-thing natural in this world has its allotted life-span. We're taught from our earliest years that death is an intrinsic part of nature, after all. But I'd better get out of here, because that bed is tempting me to hasten your ac-ceptance quite considerably.'

'Acceptance?' she echoed tartly, although she was struggling with the strange rage of the wounded in re-sponse to this confirmation of his ingrained cynicism.

'Decision, then,' he amended equably.

'My decision is already made, Simon,' Fee advised him pointedly.

'There in your heart, since you're into the concept,' he agreed, touching her lightly just below the left breast, and she flinched away from him.

'Only I never even considered the alternative,' she supplemented sharply.

'Your head will catch up with your heart,' he assured her, his smile scintillating. 'I'm looking forward to having you around the office—being able to witness the process, getting to know you better, watching you getting to know me.'

'I haven't said I'm taking the job yet,' Fee flared, her chin lifting rebelliously. 'I won't be rushed.'

'No, and I'll never try to rush you, Fee—in any way,' Simon added meaningfully, his charm outrageously evident just then. 'That's one advantage to all this—the fact that we do already know each other fairly well, so there will be fewer adjustments than usual to be made on both sides. For instance, I know you too well to im-agine that an attempt to sweep you off your feet, or pressure you, wouldn't rebound against me. You react negatively to that sort of thing, don't you, and particularly right now when you're so ferociously into autonomy, determined to make your own decisions? I suppose all this rather desperate independence is your response to life with Sheldon, if he tried to do your thinking for you, which it sounds like. That reminds me! This isn't the first time he has contacted you like that, is it? If you want to spare yourself his particular brand of bullying in future, I suggest you always let one of the others answer the phone while you remain here, and don't pick it up if it rings when you're on your own.'

'I'd already thought of that for myself.'

Because nothing else she had so far come up with had succeeded in deterring the man.

Fee's expression was closed, concealing the inner desperation that accompanied the reflection, and Simon surveyed her pensively for a moment.

'Don't worry, sweetheart. You really are quite safe here. I'll be seeing you.'

The strange thing was that she really did feel better—safer—now that Simon knew about the calls, she realised when he had gone.

It was because he was so dynamically able, she decided. You couldn't imagine anyone, even a man as powerful as Vance Sheldon was, getting away with anything Simon didn't want him to do. Even if he tried, Simon would find a way of stopping him—or so it had seemed, but the conviction was beginning to fade now that he had gone, because she knew perfectly well that he would never really put himself to any trouble on another's behalf.

It seemed incredible that a man like Simon should be interested in her as a woman, that he should find her attractive, but she had to accept it. Twice today, he had kissed her so——

Fee couldn't think of an appropriate word. The skill, the expertise for which he was famed, had been there, but it had also been so nice—his word—she decided, falling back on the prosaic.

She knew his interest wouldn't last. At present, she was a novelty; he was contrasting her with the teenager he had known, but he would soon start looking at her with more cynical eyes and discover that she lacked both the physical attributes and the personality of the women who usually attracted him. He was probably going through a phase when his romantic and sexual appetite was jaded, and the first truly stunning woman who crossed his path was sure to revive it, but in the meantime he was turning to the unusual and the idiosyncratic in the hope of finding stimulation and distraction.

The thought of her response to Simon made her squirm, however, as there was simply no acceptable explanation. There had so seldom been a need privately to rationalise or justify any of her behaviour in the past that she lacked the knack, completely at a loss. Of course, she had never been oblivious to his physical perfection, nor his outward charm, she admitted, so perhaps it had been mere curiosity.

Curiosity. It was the best she could come up with. She had wanted to know what all those other women had felt—except that she could never feel exactly as they had because she had seen too many of them, seen them suffer, and she knew Simon too well to be in any danger of falling in love with him herself.

Thus she reflected that she could probably quite safely risk accepting the job at Rhodes Properties, even if he persisted in viewing her as the next woman in his life, as he had so casually phrased it. At least he would never be devious about his interest in the way that Vance Sheldon had been.

She could trust him, and as for trusting herself—Fee finally decided that she could. She wasn't conceited or complacent, but neither was she stupid or self-destructive. Simon was a devastatingly attractive man, magnificently male, and she had responded physically to the fact, but she knew herself to be the opposite of promiscuous, although she had learnt to conceal the private idealism that shaped her—no heroic voice of innocence, she—shrinking sensitively from the contempt in which so many people seemed to hold her conviction that attraction and love ought to be inseparable. She had never judged those who differed from her, but in the secrecy of her heart she was convinced that sex divorced from love had to be horrifying and degrading, a tawdry sham that mocked what it imitated.

A little later, discovering she was hungry, Fee slipped downstairs and helped herself to some of the risotto she found being kept warm. Leaving the kitchen again, she was aware of a draught of fresh air coming from somewhere, cool and clean after the rain, and she paused, looking into the lounge as a lazy murmur of masculine voices came to her.

The lounge itself was in darkness, although the doors to the patio stood open and a light was on out there. There was no sign of Babs, but she could see Simon and Charles, each with a glass in his hand, and one of them must just have cracked a joke because they were both laughing, and it was the sort of laughter in which men seldom indulged when women were present.

Fee shook her head and retreated quietly, wanting to feel disgusted but finding herself more inclined to be amused. They were probably intent on getting drunk together in the way that men periodically set out to do, for no apparent good reason save that they felt like it.

She didn't understand men and their rituals. Sometimes they seemed like an alien species altogether, instead of the other half of her own kind, but she imagined that women with more experience than she herself possessed had developed some sort of sketchy understanding of their strange ways.

If he wasn't working or seeing Loren Kincaid tonight, she supposed Simon might simply have been reluctant to go home too early. Even someone as insensitive as he was must occasionally dread the prospect of solitude, and, despite possessing the sort of super-intelligence which often voluntarily chose isolation in preference to intellectually inferior company, Simon was a sociable man. He liked people even if they did all bore him eventually, clever and stupid alike.

He would revert to finding her boring, and sooner rather than later, Fee hoped. His interest was just too disturbing.

By the time Miss Sung-Li contacted her with a formal offer of the position as Simon's personal assistant, Fee had made up her mind.

She listened to the older woman outlining the terms of the standard Rhodes Properties contract, which she realised was admirable, as binding on them as employers as it would be on her, safeguarding both parties, while the list of benefits she would enjoy as an employee was impressive.

But the safeguards she required couldn't be written into an agreement. If it were only the job, she would have accepted without even hearing Miss Sung-Li out, but there was Simon himself to be taken into consideration. She had no illusions about his difficult nature and lacerating tongue, but she wasn't quite as sensitive as she had been four years ago when his anger or impatience could virtually destroy her.

It was his new attitude towards her that kept her silent, trying to find the courage to say what she needed to.

She didn't like Simon, and she had her own dreams and desires, immensely different from his, but she did find him disturbing. He was attractive, he could be charming and amusing at times, and when he had kissed her she had been prey to that terrible, vulnerable, melting sensation. That was what she didn't want to have to feel again.

Fee bit her lip, experiencing a slight surge of resentment, because why should she have to be hesitating about accepting a definitely alluring position just because Simon currently had some whim about her?

It was this reflection that finally made her brave enough to say, 'I know this is an unusual request, Miss Sung-Li, but before I definitely accept the job *I* want to interview Mr Rhodes.'

There was a substantial pause before Miss Sung-Li said slowly, 'It's more than unusual, it's unprecedented, Miss Garland, but I have to assume that you're sufficiently well acquainted with Mr Rhodes to be confident that he'll find it acceptable. We'll make a provisional appointment and I'll get back to you and confirm it when I've obtained his approval.'

As she replaced the receiver, Fee was smiling slightly, partly with relief but also because she was realising that the confidence in her own judgement, which had deserted her on realising how wrong she had been about Vance Sheldon, must be beginning to reassert itself. Her courage too, she thought, feeling happier than she had done in weeks.

Perhaps she could cope with Simon.

Nevertheless, she was tense and a little nervous as Miss Sung-Li herself escorted her up to Simon's suite of offices the following morning, but she thought that was natural enough in the circumstances.

Then a wave of sympathy temporarily washed everything else away as they entered the outer office and she

saw Maynah Norman at the desk which would become
hers if she accepted the job. Whatever the outcome of
this interview, at least she wouldn't end up like Maynah.

When the blonde girl announced their presence to
Simon, the door of his office was flung open almost
immediately.

'Fee! Thank you, Miss Sung-Li,' he added with his
most blazing smile.

Fee's heart and pulses had jumped as he appeared and
she was aware of the inevitable effect of his presence.
She felt alive, alert, perceptions and senses heightened,
as if he reached out and shared his vitality with her.

'Thank you.' She smiled at Miss Sung-Li who inclined
her head and departed.

Simon seemed to be in a good mood and he stood
looking at Fee for a moment, warm blue eyes sweeping
over her face and her simple outfit of a slim white skirt
worn beneath a soft dark pink collarless jacket with
three-quarter sleeves and pretty vertical pleat detail at
the front.

'Come through,' he invited her, closing the door when
they were in the office. 'How are you? Sit down. Miss
Sung-Li says you want to interview me, which is quite
a novelty. What can I tell you? What do you want to
know?'

He was so vibrant with energy and he spoke so fast
that Fee felt slightly breathless as she took one of the
chairs in front of his desk, which she had recognised as
a valuable piece of furniture despite its simplicity.

'I don't so much want information as to...' She hesitated as he sat down opposite her.

'To lay down some rules?' he suggested mockingly,
his quick mind characteristically leaping ahead.

'Something like that,' she acknowledged drily, and a
gleam appeared in his eyes. 'The details don't concern

you but, you see, I didn't particularly like the way things ended up with Mr Sheldon——'

'Yes, I'd say you made a mistake there,' Simon inserted arrogantly.

'—and since now *you've* chosen to imagine that there's something personal between us——'

'It's hardly my imagination, darling,' Simon drawled with indolent good humour, but then his expression hardened. 'I'm not Sheldon, Fee, if that's the reassurance you're looking for... Has he tried to phone you again, by the way?'

'No, or not that I know of.' Fee's face clouded. 'The others have been answering all calls and I don't think they'd tell me if he had in case it upset me.'

'No, they wouldn't. They do believe in protecting you, don't they?' Just for a moment, there was a tense look about his mouth before he smiled at her. 'All right, Fee, in view of what has passed between us recently, I suppose it's understandable that you should want to know exactly where you stand. I'm not going to mislead you. The more I think about it, the more I'm sold on the idea of your being the next woman in my private life—but our working relationship will be just that, and even if you should happen to reject me in our private relationship you won't find our working one suddenly made intolerable for you, which, if I'm reading the lines correctly, seems to have been Sheldon's initial reaction to your ending the affair, even if he now regrets it... So does all this satisfy you, or is there something else?'

Fee met his eyes. 'I didn't need to hear those particular things, Simon. I know you'd never behave like Mr Sheldon. You're much too civilised and...self-respecting.'

'Well, that bodes well for the future.' Simon saw her expression tighten in response to the lightly flirtatious tone, and he laughed. 'Is that it, then? You don't want me to even refer to our personal relationship-to-be? That's asking a hell of a lot, Fee. You know me, you know what I'm like, how I talk. I'm accustomed to expressing myself as and when something occurs to me, not to curbing myself—although I am already exercising more restraint with you than I do with other women, just because you are so different and, as I've said before, I know sweeping you off your feet would be a mistake. No, I can't promise never to *refer* to personal matters, but we can separate our professional and personal relationships in every other way. I've always done that quite successfully anyway. It has never been a problem, separating the two sides of my life.'

'No, because one is just light entertainment to you, isn't it, you can take it or leave it?' she prompted tartly.

'Are you calling me cold?' He was amused. 'I'm not, as you will find out for yourself, but I can control myself, Fee, and I do promise you that there will be no actual harassment as such, no sexual or emotional blackmail or intimidation. Does that satisfy you?'

'I suppose it will have to.'

Because she had only just realised how very much she wanted this job. Working with Simon would be an adventure; a test too, but all the perils she had to face would be there on the bright surface, not lurking below in darkness as they had proved to be in her previous job. Fee gave him a contained smile.

'Right, those are your conditions dealt with,' Simon said. 'Now mine.'

CHAPTER FIVE

SIMON'S tone had been overtly challenging and, leaving Fee no time to react, he went on to specify, 'I reserve the right to appreciate you as a woman, not some sexless automaton; to look at you and admire you and to say so—for instance, if I think you're looking particularly nice, I'll tell you, and I shall expect you to accept it in the spirit it's meant. You are looking lovely now, in fact... I can't stand those women who hear sexual innuendo in every innocent compliment and suspect every accidental or unthinking touch of being a prelude to a pounce.'

'And how precisely do we identify the dividing line?' Fee demanded tautly. 'Some women err on the other side, by being insufficiently suspicious.'

As she herself had done not so long ago, she reflected, some of her lingering bitterness revealing itself in the angry sparkle of her eyes and the momentary tightening of her sensitive mouth. Never again, she had promised herself, even if it meant the suppression of her natural instinct, which was to accept people at face value—believe the best, take them on trust.

She had even ignored things that had made her uneasy, making excuses for Mr Sheldon, reluctant to be like those women Simon had just been decrying, and look how she had ended up—a subject of public speculation, humiliated and embarrassed.

In future, she had promised herself, she would question every single thing that struck her as out of line or threatening, and particularly if it came from her boss.

However alien it might be to her peaceful nature, she had to adopt the sort of aggressiveness that would cause people—men—to think twice about trying to take advantage of her, whether emotionally or physically.

Simon was looking thoughtful in response to her words.

'Yes, I do recognise that you have a valid point there,' he conceded. 'But you have to agree that there's a lot of over-reaction too. It's no wonder there are so many wimps around. Men are being emasculated.'

'Not you,' Fee asserted unthinkingly, then shut her mouth smartly, realising that commenting on his undoubted masculinity hardly constituted practicing what she was attempting to preach.

Simon was laughing at her.

'It's all right, you're allowed to break the rules all you like. I'm only distracted when I want to be so I'll be only too delighted,' he added softly, and paused, looking at her enquiringly. 'So, Fee? Are you going to work for me?'

'Yes,' she committed herself simply.

Satisfaction made his eyes bluer than ever.

'Of course, everything I've just undertaken to do, or not to do, applies to business hours only,' he cautioned her candidly. 'Away from work, the rules change, but there again, we'll keep the two sides separate, because if we end up sharing our nights there'll be no room for work.'

He was outrageous and Fee spluttered, trying to restrain a spontaneous gasp of laughter.

'Away from work, I don't have to have anything to do with you.' She was emphatic.

'Except that we happen to belong to overlapping social circles,' he cautioned her amusedly, not at all affronted by her rejection. 'But I take it that means you don't want me to come along and help you choose an apartment from that list I gave you?'

'Why should I?' Fee retorted with a razor-sharp little smile. 'I've already turned down a similar offer from Babs.'

She had been tempted to reject his list, but it was probably over-reacting to suspect him of undue interference there, and in fact two of the places on it sounded so attractive that now that she had this job she meant to lose no time contacting the residential division to find out when she could view them.

'Ah, but Babs would be pointing out all the drawbacks, pouring cold water all over your enthusiasm and trying to persuade you to stay safely at home with her and Charles—that woman really should have a child of her own—whereas I'd be encouraging you to go for whatever appealed to you,' Simon asserted on a teasing note, eyes brilliant with enjoyment. 'Choosing a home is more fun if you've got someone sharing the experience with you.'

'Which of your girlfriends helped you choose your house, or can't you remember?' Fee returned, eyes limpid with assumed innocence.

Belatedly, she realised that once again she was forgetting her own rules. Why couldn't she remain impersonal? Why this interest in a private life she deplored?

His face had hardened perceptibly. 'None, as you know very well. Most women seem to view an invitation to go house-hunting as a simultaneous invitation to share the house.'

'And you prefer to occupy yours in solitary splendour,' she taunted.

But Simon had relaxed again, shrugging dismissively and smiling. 'In fact, I don't often get the opportunity to spend much time in it.'

'Too much work or too many women?' she mocked
sweetly. 'What a full, busy life you must lead, Simon.'

But was there any richness or depth to it? Clearly,
though, he cherished the privacy of his home, even if
he only chose to make use of it occasionally, so perhaps
there were other, more thoughtful facets to him, ones
his business associates, employees and social acquaintances never saw.

Her derision merely seemed to amuse him, although
she was also aware of an alert sparkle of interest in his
eyes as he regarded her.

'It seems to trouble you—— Wait, I get it! Relax, Fee.
I thought you knew. I have a very strict rule—one woman
at a time.'

And, for the time being, he was amusing himself by
speculating about the possibility of making her Loren
Kincaid's successor, blithely ignoring the fact that to do
so he would need her co-operation.

Fee's face was shuttered. She would just have to find
a way of dealing with him out of the office if he kept it
up—which she still didn't believe he would. She had only
to refuse to see him privately.

As for their working relationship, she thought she
could cope, if only she could conquer this annoying urge
to get under his skin and find a more sensitive, complex
Simon than the man she really knew him to be.

'I have been warned,' she acknowledged tartly.

'Well, it was meant to be reassuring, really.' But the
look Simon gave her remained distinctly predatory for
a few seconds, before altering. 'There's the matter of
your contract. Miss Sung-Li will be getting someone to
organise it. She has discussed salary and benefit schemes
with you, hasn't she? I hope she warned you that I'm a
demanding boss and expect perfection, but I do realise
that you'll have to learn as you go along as Maynah
won't be here to tell you how we do things. She wants

to leave today if possible, so you could tell her she can go, and start as soon as you've seen the people in our legal department if you like.'

Fee's eyes sparkled as she stood up, and he followed suit. 'If that's what you want. Then I'll go down now, while you thank Maynah and say goodbye.'

Simon looked startled, but then a smile flitted across his face. 'Was I sounding boorish? Yes, of course I should. She has been an excellent assistant, but the annoyance of knowing I'd have to replace her has tended to make me lose sight of that lately. In the end, though, it hasn't been such a hassle after all. Charles did me a favour.'

'You don't know that yet,' Fee cautioned him, reluctantly amused by his satisfaction.

'Oh, but I do, Fee, I do.'

Working for Simon, Fee discovered fascinating new facets of his personality. He was a man who enjoyed his work intensely, meeting its challenges with zest and openly revelling in his successes.

He was a demanding man to work for, but he was generally reasonable and, as Miss Sung-Li had once mentioned, he asked even more of himself than he did of those he employed. Within days, Fee shared her fellow-employees' respect for him, although she was aware that their consequent loyalty didn't prevent their speculating avidly and enjoyably about his notorious private life. It was natural. She frequently wondered herself.

Secretly, Fee was glad that that side existed and that she had personally observed so much of it, because it kept her from respecting the whole man, something she felt instinctively that it would be dangerous to do, the first step towards liking him.

Of course, even as a boss, he wasn't perfect, although she found his major faults understandable, his impatience with those who stated the obvious or the unnecessary, and that tendency he had in common with other clever people to forget that not everyone shared his quick, logical thought processes, assuming that if he knew how he wanted something done whoever was to do it automatically understood too.

'You hadn't explained to him,' Fee ventured quietly once when a young man from Rents and Levies hadn't produced what was required promptly enough for Simon's liking because he had needed to get back to Fee for elaboration.

'Hadn't I?' Simon was honestly surprised. 'I thought he knew. He's usually excellent at his job.'

'Most people are if they know what's wanted,' she retorted, and he laughed before looking thoughtful.

'Yes, of course. It's a bad habit of mine and I do try, but I keep forgetting.' Pausing, he regarded her enquiringly. 'Do you think I expect too much of people, Fee?'

'Not too much, but a lot,' she submitted, not sure why he was asking.

'It's only in a working environment, though.' Strangely, he seemed to be offering some sort of reassurance. 'Away from work, I don't think I expect a lot.'

'Hardly anything at all,' Fee agreed a little tartly, recalling particularly his conviction concerning the transitory nature of love. 'Because that way you'll never be disappointed, will you?'

'Have you been disappointed?' Simon ignored the audible taunt.

'Often,' she admitted simply, knowing she would probably go on being disappointed by people all her life, despite her recent resolve to be a lot less trusting.

'Because you expect too much.' Simon was infuriatingly superior.

'Because I'm not a cynic like you.'

Her retort seemed to fascinate him briefly, and he spent several seconds examining her expression before abruptly abandoning the personal and becoming businesslike once more.

As usual, Fee found it disconcerting. On one level she was getting to know Simon better, seeing him daily like this, and yet in a personal sense he had become utterly elusive, although whether because he was adhering to the rules they had laid down for their working relationship or because—as was all too likely—he had lost interest in her, either having met someone new or found that he wasn't ready to part with Loren yet, she wasn't sure.

It was not knowing for sure that she found so frustrating, Fee supposed, and yet she shrunk from probing, half afraid of the answer.

Simon no longer even seemed interested in her need to find a flat. In the end she had settled on one of the two that had attracted her on his list, inevitably the most expensive because it was out of the high-rise districts and one of only four in a small double-storey block built on a rise overlooking Repulse Bay, not far from where Babs and Charles lived, a fact which had helped reconcile Babs to Fee's insistence on being independent.

They had hired a truck for a weekend to transport the furniture Fee had chosen from a surplus in the house, much of it belonging to her father, who she knew would have no objection.

Even when Simon required her to work late on the Friday she refrained from admitting that she would have preferred not to that particular night, quietly getting on with the job that had cropped up, resigning herself to only starting the move the following day, and gratefully aware that it was only because Rhodes Properties paid her so well that she was going to be living in sight of green hills and blue sea, rather than surrounded by concrete towers.

'Do you need a lift home?' Simon asked her, almost indifferently, when she was finally free to leave.

'No, thank you, there'll still be plenty of buses and fourteen-seater taxis running,' she rejected the offer politely.

'Can you come in tomorrow morning?' he added with more interest in this question than his previous one. 'We could get on with the final proposals for the Macau project.'

'Sorry, I can't. Any other Saturday, but not this one.'

She knew she was within her rights, especially as the Macau proposals, which they had planned to deal with on Monday, weren't needed until the end of the following week, and her contract with Rhodes Properties stipulated mutual flexibility where Saturdays were concerned.

Simon shrugged, accepting it with a derisive curl of his lips. 'I suppose it was inevitable that you'd revert to round-eye vices in Australia. Weekends are sacred!'

'This one is, anyway,' she returned coolly, irrationally piqued when he let her go without trying to find out what she had planned, and then furious with herself when her mind caught up with her emotions.

What was the matter with her? She didn't want Simon to be interested in her. She wasn't interested in him.

Charles had driven back to the house for the last of the furniture and other items Fee wanted, leaving her alone to arrange or put away what he had just brought, when Simon came strolling in through the open door of the little upstairs flat late the following afternoon, making her jump nervously. She was suddenly acutely aware of the brief pink shorts she wore beneath a black shirt of fine, soft cotton, and she hated herself for being so self-conscious.

'Charles says he won't be long,' Simon advised her, sparing her long, slender legs a casual glance before turning his attention to her face. 'I dropped in at the house to find out what you were up to. You didn't tell me you were moving today.'

'You didn't ask,' she responded shortly, and then wondered what she had betrayed when she saw his bland smile.

'You laid down the rules for our working relationship, darling,' he reminded her smoothly. 'I'm not supposed to express a personal interest in you, am I? But I'm not as rigid as you. If ever you want to volunteer personal information, go right ahead, I won't mind.'

'Well, not right now,' Fee returned flippantly, tugging ineffectually at a small bookshelf. 'I'm busy, as you can see.'

'Let me do that. Where do you want it?' The book-shelf in place, he looked round, his expression growing slightly complacent. 'I had a feeling this was the place you'd choose.'

'It was the built-in barbecue that persuaded me,' Fee mentioned, needing an excuse to step out on to the balcony, suddenly feeling oddly overwhelmed by his presence, his personality so vibrant that the apartment seemed too small to contain it.

Simon laughed, following her out. 'Aren't they supposed to be becoming *passé*? Outdoor pizza ovens were taking over last time I investigated residential trends, but there's probably something else by now... How did you persuade Babs to let you go?'

Fee's heart gave an odd angry lurch as she looked at him. He was casually dressed in an open-necked shirt with the sleeves rolled up and matching stone-coloured jeans. Fine gold hairs glinted on his forearms against the deeper gold of his tanned skin, and she lifted her eyes to his face hastily, disconcerted by the warm, vulnerable feeling that had swept through her.

The amusement she found in the bright blue eyes strengthened her again.

'Don't make fun of Babs! She's only like that because she's kind, she cares about me, and she got into the habit of mothering me when we were little and poor Angie was never around.'

She had turned to face the balcony railing, looking out over the shining bay, and Simon came to stand beside her, too close for mental comfort.

He said curiously, 'You always believe the best of people, or at least take the charitable view, don't you? Why?'

'Because it's usually true.' It was a slip, the creed a remnant of her old trusting beliefs, because she kept forgetting the new, cautious—suspicious person she wanted to be, so, with some idea of neutralising it, she added antagonistically, 'Except of you, probably, Simon. What do you want?'

'Don't rage at me, darling,' Simon drawled, his hands resting lightly on the top of the railing. 'I've just spent an incredibly boring and frustrating afternoon, trying to make the parting of the ways easy on Loren. Did I have to do it that indirect way? Couldn't I have been honest with the girl, put her out of her misery once and for all?'

'Why are you asking me?' Fee demanded sharply. 'Don't try to make me an accessory to your bad behaviour. It's none of my business how you conduct your affairs. It has nothing to do with me.'

'You know it has everything to do with you, Fee,' he contradicted her quite softly, but she saw his expression harden with resolve. 'And to please you I was trying

to be subtle about getting rid of a superfluous...
attachment, let's call it, since what you've termed my
brutality upsets you so much, although personally I still
believe quick and clean is the best way. I might as well
tell you I had to do it that way with Loren in the end.
She didn't understand anything else. I didn't mention
you, although she'll have to know eventually. Already
she's convinced it's someone I met at your welcome-home
party. Anyway, I won't be seeing her again.'

'But what are you doing it all *for*, Simon?' Fee asked,
making it very pointed.

'To uncomplicate my love life,' he taunted. 'You
wouldn't want me while I was still involved with another
woman, would you? I don't believe in it myself anyway.
I may start seeing someone new while I'm still involved
elsewhere, but I never actually start a new affair until
I've formally ended the previous one.'

'Oh, very moral and upright of you. I don't want you,
full stop, Simon!' She heard her voice lift with frustration. 'I don't even like you, and even if I did I do
like myself too much to want to be one of a number.
Do you even know how many affairs you've had in your
life?'

'Probably not nearly as many as people imagine, because while I always look and always will, even when
I'm ninety, I don't always touch.' His gaze had grown
sharp as he half turned towards her. 'But I see what's
worrying you. No, Fee, I can't give you the number of
my affairs offhand, but I've always been careful. There
has never been any risk involved—ever.'

'Yes, I think I've always guessed that,' she accepted
seriously. 'You're too...together, too fond of yourself
for anything less.'

'Respect and consideration for the women concerned
also comes into it,' he emphasised gently before grinning

irrepressibly. 'Not to mention my total and annihilating fear of being caught in women's favourite trap.'

'I'm sure you'd get out of it somehow,' she predicted waspishly, resentment rising. 'But the whole question is irrelevant here. Where's this famous respect and consideration when you break their hearts?'

'Oh, Fee.' Simon showed her empty hands, the gesture wryly helpless. 'What can I say? You know I can't promise eternal devotion—— Oh hell, I never mean to break their hearts, and I'm sure they all get over it eventually. Love doesn't last... But if you and I get together, I can only swear I'll try not to hurt you, and you do know me, so you'll know what to expect. I'll never cause you any distress——'

'What are you doing now, then?' she asked caustically.

'At least I haven't distressed you by letting anyone else know there's a personal side to our relationship yet,' he pointed out coolly. 'I do know how much you'd hate that at this stage, while your old prejudice against me still exists.'

Fee hesitated. She supposed that, from Simon, such discretion was almost uniquely considerate, but she wasn't sure if she believed the reason he had given for it.

'And it has nothing to do with not wanting to look stupid yourself when you either lose interest or...or have to accept defeat?'

It seemed incredible that she should be saying these things to Simon—of all people. When had he ever been defeated, by anyone? So what hope had she? Oh, he would lose interest soon.

A spark of wicked enjoyment showed itself in his eyes. 'But I'm not going to be defeated, Fee.'

'All right, I suppose I should be grateful,' she offered grudgingly, not really inclined to believe he was being so reticent out of consideration for her, and resentment resurfaced as she reminded herself that there was no need to worry about the possibility of having hurt his feelings when everyone knew he didn't have any. 'I know only too well just how badly you can embarrass people—how thorough public humiliation at your hands can be.'

'Are you referring to yourself or others?'

Abruptly, his voice was freezing, reminding her just how ruthless he could be, and Fee shivered inwardly although she thought perhaps it was a sign that he was already becoming bored, probably because she had just shown her ignorance of the rules by which he liked to play his games. The women he was used to either flirted wittily or were so overwhelmed, they adored dumbly.

'Oh, forget it.' She dismissed the question, wanting to come across as coolly indifferent, only it came out sounding defiant. 'It's irrelevant here because it's not prejudice, as you've just called it, Simon, but actual, factual knowledge.'

The ensuing silence was unnerving. She could feel Simon studying her, the relentless weight of his attention heating her skin.

Finally, though, he laughed.

'You do believe in looking on the down side, don't you, darling?' he taunted slightly. 'All right, I know you're probably a bit wary since you claim to have spent your life stumbling over women in floods of tears because of me—which I beg leave to doubt, incidentally— but do be realistic. If you think about it, I've managed to stay friends with most of the women I've been involved with, one way or another. Ismay Compton, for instance. They've got over me, forgiven me.'

'There's no point in any of this,' Fee snapped. 'Because I don't like you, and some of the time I think I really hate you——'

'Then why did you kiss me the way you did?'

'Some kind of stupid chemistry, I suppose.' She was conscious of sounding a shade too defensive.

'Well, isn't that what all this is about anyway?' Simon prompted amusedly.

'It hasn't lasted, though,' Fee added bitingly.

'No?'

He lifted a hand from the balcony railing and she shivered slightly as she felt the back of his fingers against her bare upper arm, rubbing lightly up and down for a moment, the gentle friction creating a warm, weak feeling.

'Just chemistry, that's all,' she insisted scathingly, angrily aware of the futility of attempting to deny her reaction to a man of Simon's experience.

'Yes, and it works both ways. Chemistry,' Simon repeated musingly as he returned his hand to the railing. 'People call it by all sorts of names—attraction, desire, love—but chemistry is really all it is.'

'Now that's really romantic!' It was drenched in sarcasm. 'If that's how you talk to your girlfriends, it's just a wonder they're still stupid enough to fall in love with you.'

'Oh, I'm quite capable of giving it other descriptions, such as being in love. It has never been a lie either.'

'But I bet it always comes with a qualification,' Fee guessed shrewdly. 'Like—for now, at this time, until you fall in love again.'

'That's only fair, surely?' Simon had seemed to be enjoying the debate, but now his face hardened and there was a ruthless diamond brilliance to his eyes. 'Only once in my life have I ever been unfair—when I was still in my teens, I suppose because I wanted to believe . . . Hell, I even made promises! She was one of my first girlfriends, and I've never forgotten how upset she was, and what a brute I felt when I had to tell her that I'd been fooling myself—and her. She had a right to be upset. None of the others has.'

'Because you've made them no promises—because you know that love doesn't last,' she derided, striving to mimic the tone in which he usually said it, suddenly and irrationally furious with him, as well as with herself, because she knew his cynical attitude shouldn't matter to her. '*How* do you know, Simon?'

'What are you so cross about?' he wondered interestedly, scrutinising her with narrowed eyes. 'I know through personal experience and scientific observation, Fee.'

'Oh, very scientific! And what personal experience?' Fee laughed angrily, although somewhere deep in her mind she was appalled to hear herself. 'You may have been *in love* a thousand times, but I don't believe you've ever *loved*!'

It held him silent for several seconds, at the end of which he gave her an ironic smile. 'No, I don't suppose I have, although I think I may have adored once.'

His tone was so complex that Fee was distracted, her rage subsiding slightly.

'What happened?' she asked involuntarily.

He shrugged dismissively. 'Oh, she's gone. I let her go.'

'That thing about letting someone go and if they love you they'll come back to you?' Inexplicably, Fee felt disturbed by the idea.

'No, nothing like that. I never expected her to come back.' His brief, reflectively brooding mood had passed, and he was smiling challengingly into her eyes. 'But we're not talking about adoration or anything like it here. Let's call it attraction, since you object to chemistry. I am attracted. I love just looking at you; the contrast between those dark curls and that fair skin, and the way the soft colour comes up into your cheeks—it's doing it now—and your eyes ... I don't think I've ever seen such a dark blue in anyone else... And your mouth, like some bright, sensitive flower——'

'Stop it,' Fee protested, in real distress now, but not really knowing why.

Simon looked at her in surprise. 'Why? Most women adore being told how lovely they are.'

That was it, of course. He had used that same tone of voice and said similar things to scores of other women.

'Just don't,' she insisted tightly.

He studied her in silence for several seconds before shrugging.

'All right.' But his brilliant, warm blue eyes sparkled in a way that she distrusted just before he glanced down at the road beneath them. 'Relax, sweetheart, here's Charlie to the rescue—and Babs has come along to check up on you too.'

They went out to help bring in the last few items of furniture and a suitcase of Fee's clothes, and then the men spent some time following Fee's directions as to where she wanted the heavier pieces of furniture, after which everyone accepted cold drinks from the compact bar-fridge Fee had borrowed from Charles and Babs until she could buy one of her own.

Babs grew anxious when Charles suggested it was time he and she were getting home as they were expecting guests.

'Why don't you come back with us, Fee? I know you got some groceries, but you won't feel like getting a proper meal for yourself after the day you've just spent, all those trips back and forth, and moving furniture around, and you need to eat after so much physical activity. You'll feel depressed all on your own because you're tired—especially after having had to work late last night,' she added with an accusing look at Simon,

who gave Fee a look that was far too bland to be
innocent.

'She won't be on her own, Barbara, and nor will she
have to feed herself. I'm taking her out to dinner, partly
in appreciation of the overtime she gave me last
night—— No, thanks,' he added as Babs began to suggest
that he also attend the dinner party. 'That won't do because I've got an ulterior motive, so we wouldn't be very
social. Since Fee couldn't also work this morning, we've
got business to discuss—that Macau interest I was telling
you about, Chas. Don't worry, Babs, I'll take care of
her and see she's safely locked in for the night when I
bring her home.'

He was watching Fee's furious face, the unholy enjoyment gleaming in his vivid eyes convincing her of his
silent inward laughter.

'I'd rather not, thank you, Simon,' she said ungra-
ciously. 'We were going to go through the Macau proposals on Monday, and, as Babs says, I've had an
exhausting day——'

'Which makes you an unfit guest for a dinner party,
and yet you need to be fed.' Simon's tone was calcu-
lating. 'And think of Babs. She's not going to be able
to relax and enjoy her evening as hostess if she's worrying
about you sitting here all on your own.'

She should have known that Simon would never fight
fair, Fee reflected bitterly. He knew how she adored Babs,
who was already looking concerned. The thought of
causing her distress and spoiling the pleasure she always
took in entertaining was bad enough; but personally she
also shrank from the prospect of the curiosity it would
excite if she went on protesting. Somehow, as Simon
rather surprisingly seemed to sense, she didn't want Babs
and Charles to know she was the current, temporary
object of his interest—because it was a humiliating position, making her one of an anonymous crowd, she de-

cided, although she didn't suppose Simon's arrogance would let him entertain that as a reason for her instinctive secrecy.

'Oh, all right,' Fee gave in helplessly, but the glance she flung at Simon was sparkling with hatred.

'Great. I'll come back and fetch you later,' Simon said.

'Warren Bates is going to be put out if he means to contact you tonight, though.' Babs had relaxed, satisfied that Fee wasn't going to be spending a solitary evening. 'I'd completely forgotten, Fee. He rang this afternoon, so I gave him your number here.'

'Be careful who else you give it to, Babs,' Simon cautioned with a slight hardening of his features as he glanced at Fee. 'Bates? That young man shows a distinct tendency to snarl at me whenever I come across him, for some strange reason.'

'He snarls for an *excellent* reason,' Fee hissed unguardedly, to which he responded with an ironically enquiring look.

'Oh, we all feel like snarling at you occasionally, Simon,' Charles joked, preventing any further response to Fee's little comment, rather to her relief.

Of course, Simon wouldn't care how much damage he had done to Warren's touchy, new-found pride when he had sent him packing at that barbecue four years ago, and he would experience no sympathy or fellow-feeling if he realised. She couldn't imagine him ever having gone through that agonising stage, even when he was first discovering romance and sex—even with that girl to whom he had confessed to making promises. He would have been as suave and self-assured in his dealings with his very first girlfriend as he was with women now, his sense of his masculine identity absolute and inviolable.

Nothing ever disconcerted Simon Rhodes.

CHAPTER SIX

'THIS absolute silence is reminiscent of the teenage Fee,' Simon commented teasingly, slanting Fee a wicked glance.

'So sorry,' she apologised sarcastically.

'Oh, I don't mind,' he assured her with one of his most devastatingly charming smiles.

It aroused her curiosity. 'I'd have thought you would.'

'Not at all, although I know you're actually sulking and the old—young—Fee is gone forever. I've got mixed feelings about that in fact, but don't let it bother you.'

He had called for her in his Rolls-Royce, the chosen car of nearly all Hong Kong's wealthy, proving that in some things he could be ultra-conventional. The restaurant to which he had brought her hadn't existed when Fee had left the Crown Colony but, although new, it was evidently already fashionable as Simon had greeted people at a couple of tables on the way in. Situated on the top floor of one of the island's skyscrapers, it was encased in glass, commanding a glittering view of the spectacular city.

Still angry, Fee had taken a minimum of trouble over her appearance, choosing to team a close-fitting black and white top with thin shoulder-straps and horizontal pleating that lay flat across her breasts and was gently gathered to dip slightly between them, with one of her trailing calf-length skirts of silky black inset with irregular lace panels.

Simon was elegant in a suit. Looking at him, Fee felt tension tightening her stomach as she reflected on nature's unfairness. With his lifestyle, he ought to have looked at least a little dissipated by now, but at thirty-three that blazing vitality of his was undimmed and still capable of making those around him feel much more alive than they did out of his presence.

It still worked even when she was furious with him, Fee discovered. There had been no chance to get this new rage out of her system yet because Simon had deliberately denied her an opportunity to get hold of him privately and tell him what she thought of him after so skilfully manipulating her into agreeing to come out to dinner, leaving her flat while Babs and Charles were still there.

But now that she had the chance to articulate her anger she found herself unable to do so, and most of the talk had come from Simon over the superb dishes and fine wines that were served to them with such civilised style and pace, alongside a compact dance-floor above which a four-piece instrumental band was now playing.

Troubling her into silence was the disturbance that had added itself to her resentment when the others had finally left her alone to reflect on what had passed between her and Simon that afternoon.

At the office, where the intensity of his absorption in work precluded all but the minimum of personal exchanges—because she couldn't flatter herself that he was really complying with the rules that seemed to amuse him so much—she could just about cope with her awareness of him, which was rapidly becoming far more acute than it had been in her teens, but this afternoon——

Of course, he was an attractive man and she responded to that, as well as to his personality—that strange mixture of the dynamic and the laid-back that made him so alertly aware of everything and yet so frustratingly imperturbable at the same time, impervious to her resentment. But the thing frightening her now went deeper.

Simon had the power to hurt her. Not in all the usual ways—she hoped—but he *had* hurt her this afternoon. There had been that inner ache, intensifying with every new proof of his entrenched cynicism where emotional matters were concerned.

He was a cynic; she had always known it. But she shouldn't *care*!

Now, putting her knife and fork together at the end of the main course, she said stiffly, 'I'm not sulking.'

'No, perhaps I used the wrong word. I don't think you're a sulker. Simmering, then? Or seething?'

'Dead right!' she confirmed with a glint in her eyes as his derision had the usual effect of summoning her fighting spirit.

'Then come and dance. Perhaps you'll calm down—or come to the boil!' he invited her laughingly.

'All right.'

Feeling challenged, as much by her own need to prove that she could remain immune to him if necessary as by his flippancy, she rose and went with him.

'So you're still cross with me,' he prompted with lazy amusement, turning her lightly into his arms as they reached the smooth dance-floor.

'I suppose you're actually proud of being so devious,' she stormed, but quietly. 'Manipulating people, manoeuvring them around like—like...'

'Pawns on a chess-board is probably the phrase you're looking for,' he supplied coolly, some of his amusement vanishing. 'No, Fee, I was not devious, so don't even suggest it again. I didn't deceive you, I didn't hide my intentions, and I made sure you knew exactly what I was doing and why, when I did my manipulating.'

'Oh, you admit to that part of it? And what about Babs and Charles?' Fee demanded tempestuously. 'They didn't know. And you call Charles your friend!'

'You can hardly expect me to have reformed completely in so short a space of time,' Simon drawled, not attempting to defend himself.

It disconcerted her, as did the discovery that she was shivering although the hand at her back was warm and so were the arms encircling her.

'Do you want to?' she questioned him warily. 'Reform?'

Simon was silent a moment. Then he laughed.

'No, not really,' he admitted. 'But I'll suppose I'll have to, at least temporarily.'

'You cynical——' Fee couldn't find appropriate words with which to express her indignation and resentment, and yet some traitorous part of her wanted to laugh just because he was so outrageously candid. 'You—I should have known. Oh, and, as you say, I did know you were manipulating me earlier, but being open and honest about it doesn't excuse you, because you knew damned well that I couldn't do anything to thwart you.'

'Without alerting the others as to what's going on,' Simon qualified it for her, a slight edge to his voice.

'Nothing is going on,' she flared antagonistically before he could continue.

'Something is. It's going on right now,' he added more softly, flattening his hand against her back, and she was aware of each individual finger and his thumb and palm, her shivering intensifying. 'But tell me, Fee, why are you so secretive about it? You can't be trying to protect them from the shock of realising that you're actually an adult, independent woman, all equipped to take care of yourself, when you've already made a statement to that effect by insisting on getting a place of your own. So what is it? Are you ashamed of the fact that I appreciate you as that woman and not just as my assistant?'

'How clever of you, Simon! Yes, that's it exactly!' Fee confirmed the charge with unusual savagery. 'Who wants to be one of a crowd? It's hardly something to be proud of!'

It was true, and yet Fee was slightly shocked at herself. She had never thought of herself as particularly special in any way, and she still found it surprising that a sophisticate like Simon should be interested in her, however casually, but at the same time she felt his interest as an insult.

'Are you implying that I'm indiscriminate where women are concerned? That's an insult to yourself as much as to me, sweetheart. In addition, I'd say I'm a damned sight more discriminating than you are in your love life. At least I keep away from married women— which makes your intolerance of my lifestyle somewhat hypocritical, don't you think? You must have known Sheldon was married when you got involved with him.'

'I've told you before, my so-called involvement with Mr Sheldon is none of your business!' Fee was angrily emphatic. 'And don't try to pretend your avoidance of married women has anything to do with morality. If it had, you wouldn't be able to believe such a thing of me so easily.'

'I might not be able to anyway, but for the *facts*, Fee,' Simon derided, eyes glinting dangerously.

'What facts?' The question was caustic. 'Just because you can boast that everything written about you in the newspapers is true—although why you should take pride in it is a mystery—it doesn't mean they get it right about everyone else every single time.'

'Oh, I accept that details can vary wildly, but the gist is generally correct. Any story is based on at least one hard fact to begin with, even if it ends up heavily embroidered.'

'It's not the embroidery that bothers me, it's the interpretation of what I suppose I have to agree are facts,' Fee snapped.

He gave her a sharp smile. 'And what interpretation do you place on the *fact* that I steer clear of married women, if you're so convinced of my lack of morality?'

Just for a second, doubt assailed her, but she suppressed it.

'You're probably just avoiding trouble,' she accused contemptuously. 'We all know you don't like having to consider anyone except yourself. And with a married woman you might have to, especially if she wanted to keep the affair secret, and she might well want to since you'd make sure she knew there was no chance of your actually replacing her husband. You've never made a sacrifice, never put yourself out for anyone, have you, Simon?'

'I've never known anyone worth putting myself out for,' he returned dismissively, impervious to her scorn. 'As for sacrifices, I've always mistrusted anyone who claims to have made them for another's sake. In fact, I have a suspicion that such claims are just a distorted form of self-congratulation.'

As always, his flippant cynicism enraged her, but at a deeper level her recognition of the emotional isolation that must be responsible for such an attitude was so appalled that she felt it as pain.

But to feel pain was to be vulnerable, she reminded herself agitatedly. She didn't want to be vulnerable to Simon—she couldn't afford to be.

So she said tartly, 'All the same, I'm a bit surprised that the idea of an illicit affair doesn't appeal to your devious mind.'

'Oh, we're back to the subject of my deviousness, are we?' Simon taunted. 'If you think about it, the deviousness was for your sake since you're so sensitive about what's between us. That's why I told Babs we had work to discuss, for instance.'

'Yes, I thought that was a lie,' Fee agreed tautly. 'So why am I here? Why did you want me to have dinner with you?'

'I've just broken up with Loren, remember?' His tone suggested that he found her question stupidly superfluous.

'Oh, right, and I'm supposed to be helping you celebrate?' Fee challenged scathingly.

'If you like. Certainly I didn't feel like spending a solitary evening . . . I can't remember when I last spent a Saturday evening alone, unless I've been working.'

He sounded slightly startled by the realisation, and Fee studied his suddenly contemplative expression with reluctant interest. They weren't so much dancing as simply swaying together, almost automatically, in time to the languid rhythm of the music, both more absorbed in what they were saying to each other than in attempting to display any prowess as dancers, although there hadn't been a single instant when Fee wasn't acutely aware of the warm physical reality of Simon as well as uncomfortably conscious of her body's hot yet shivery response to his nearness. When he had first taken her in his arms, she hadn't known what to do with her hands, but they had found their natural resting place of their own accord after a while and now lay curled loosely against his chest.

'Don't you like being alone?' she asked gravely.

Simon remained thoughtful, considering the question.

'I never have to be if I don't want to, so when I am it's from choice,' he answered her dismissively eventually. 'And I am occasionally, at home. I've got a couple called

Deng looking after the house and garden and security, that sort of thing, but the unit in which they live is separate from the house.'

The fact that he had obviously never given the subject much thought before disturbed Fee for some odd reason.

'But aren't you ever afraid that you might end up— lonely...one day?' she ventured hesitantly, despite an unnerving suspicion that it was dangerous to care, and Simon's eyes grew hard.

'Don't you start, Fee. I get enough of it from other women, the missionary types out to convert me, and naturally every one of them sees herself as the woman who is going to save me from loneliness. I don't want that from you, and I didn't expect it, frankly. You know me too well.'

It was Simon at his most ruthless, brutally rejecting her concern, and Fee felt herself wilting—shrivelling— until anger restored her.

'It seems to me that *you* don't know *me* at all, Simon, if you can imagine I was asking out of...out of some sort of self-interested motive,' she asserted tightly. 'But I'll admit that it was a really fatuous question, considering that you're right, I do know you... You'll never have to be lonely because you'll always be able to attract women, even when you're old.'

'And you're the woman I'm interested in attracting at present,' Simon quipped in response, and paused, amusement beginning to curve his lips. 'My God, I believe you really were worrying about me! It's kind of you, Fee, but wholly unnecessary, so don't.'

'I won't,' she snapped. 'Ever again.'

'Anyway, I'm glad you've stopped thinking of me as being old *already*,' he went on lightly, although he hadn't yet relaxed completely again. 'Oh, I know you only talked like that to annoy me, but it made you seem younger and less experienced than you are. Incidentally, talking of age and youth, where does Bates fit into your life? Is he really interested in you again, hoping to take up where you left off?'

'How would I know?' Fee was still taut with anger which the question exacerbated, serving as a reminder of what he had once done to her and Warren. 'Apart from a couple of phone calls, I've only seen him once, at the party, when you can hardly expect him to have been in a sociable mood, finding himself in the same room as you, and then when we went outside to talk you came and interrupted. We barely had a chance to say anything to each other.'

'It sounds as if he's shaping up to asking you out, although he seems to be a slow mover.' Simon's smile was stinging. 'Just as well, because he'll have to wait this time around. It's my turn now.'

It was offensive, and Fee's colour rose, while her legs seemed suddenly made of wood, her instinctive obedience to the slow beat of the music lost.

'I'd like to go back to the table, please,' she said stiltedly after an uncontrolled step.

'In a minute or two,' Simon promised her, pulling her a little closer. 'Relax. I'm enjoying holding you in my arms, and I intend to go on enjoying it for a while... savouring the sensation. Don't talk. Then you might enjoy it too.'

Fee had perforce to obey that last command simply because emotion was constricting her throat now. She didn't know why she had let him upset her like this. It had just been Simon, being typically Simon; she knew him well enough not to let him get to her in that way. She ought to be utterly indifferent to anything he said and did, but it seemed that she was no more immune to him now than she had been in her teens. He still invariably disturbed and infuriated.

Simon's hand had moved up beneath the silken fall of her hair. Her top left her shoulders and upper back bare, and his fingers were stroking lightly over her smooth skin, inscribing tiny circles, gently massaging, and Fee was conscious of a tender sensation unfurling deep within her, a sweet warmth that began to seep through her body in a slow honeyed tide. It was an acutely vulnerable feeling, because she seemed to be trembling inwardly as well as outwardly now, and she had an odd sense of herself as a vessel, receptive, absorbing, because Simon was responsible for all this sensation, introducing it to her, a magician's potion that worked on her intended passivity, turning it to awareness and response.

Snatching a shaky breath into her lungs, Fee looked into the handsome golden face just a little above hers. His expression was slightly remote now, yet intent, as if he was absorbing with his senses some silent information, perhaps the message of his body—or hers?

That absorbed, almost withdrawn look filled her with an aching uncertainty. How could she ever know what he was feeling and thinking? How could anyone? He gave so little of himself away, his conversation usually as civilised but superficial as the life he lived, the only real feelings he occasionally revealed such things as irritation, anger and impatience, and those all essentially the product of his intellect rather than his emotions.

Oh, and why was she thinking along such stupid lines? Simon *was* superficial; no real, deep feeling existed behind the façade or he couldn't live as he did. What you saw was what you got, all there was, and this yearning conviction that there had to be more was sheer wishful thinking.

Why should she want there to be more anyway, or even care if the façade really was a shield? She didn't like him, and, as for the way he was making her feel now, she ought not to let it trouble her too much. Simon was a handsome, sexy man, possessing in abundance all the complementary qualities that made those two things irresistible—charm, ability, power, success and intelligence. They all added up to glamour. Also, he knew how to hold a woman and touch her in a way that made her feel more feminine than she had ever done before, his skill and assurance diabolically effective. He had had enough practice after all, with so many women he couldn't give the number of his affairs, but, considering how unfairly blessed he was in most other ways, he had probably been born with that particular talent as well.

'Simon——' Fee stopped herself because her voice had a gasping, drowning quality, and she knew she couldn't manage a cool request to return to their table.

'Things to come, Fee,' Simon murmured whimsically.

'No.' Even that short word sounded ragged, and desperate.

'Yes, because it's happening for you too, isn't it, my darling? You're lovely,' he went on musingly. 'So slim . . . slender that you feel fragile, as if I've got something breakable in my hands, and it makes me want to make love to you very slowly and gently, for a long, long time.'

Words too, Fee reflected bitterly. They formed part of the magic he used on women—evocative, seductive words. A quiver of feeling accompanied his hand as it skimmed down the length of her delicate spine, coming to rest lightly at the small of her back, gently urging her closer.

'Stop it!' she demanded sharply, feeling almost frantic, terrified by the physical vulnerability he was creating so casually.

'How can I when you're so desirable?'

'How can you not, when I've asked you to?' she retorted waspishly.

'Ah! She credits me with some gentlemanly principles,' Simon joked irrepressibly.

'I credit you with your normal share of masculine pride,' she corrected him smartly. 'Because I'm sorry to have to tell you this, Simon—but you were wrong, I'm not enjoying this at all. I don't want to dance with you any more.'

'No.' His smile vanished abruptly, leaving his face unusually taut. 'I don't think I can go on dancing with you either, my darling. But on the other hand I'm not such a gentleman that I'm going to pretend to believe you and refrain from calling you a liar. You were enjoying it, Fee.'

'I——'

Her relief as he released her was fleeting, her face stiffening as she intercepted the interested looks of a couple who were dancing close by.

'What's wrong?' But Simon saw for himself and curiosity sharpened his gaze. 'You really do hate attention, don't you? God, that Australian business must have been a nightmare for you... And yet you brought it on yourself by choosing to pick your final quarrel with Sheldon in that Perth hotel, with the Press on the scene. Why the hell didn't you wait until you were safely back in whatever love-nest you used in Sydney? I suppose this dislike of being stared at means I can't even give you an affectionate peck on the cheek as befits an old family friend until we're on our own.'

'Since I don't believe you feel anything like affection for me, why would you want to?' Fee rallied, helped by the amused note in his voice, and telling herself that she was being over-sensitive when the couple were strangers, because it was quite natural for people to stare at Simon Rhodes and wonder who he was with, whether they recognised him or not, simply because he was such a magnificently vital and beautiful man.

'You're right there,' Simon conceded laughingly and ushered her back to the table.

To her relief, he left personal subjects alone, talking about his plans for the expansion of Rhodes Properties, the industrial and commercial sites he was in the final stage of acquiring in Macau, and his hopes concerning Singapore.

'That should be relatively easy but, as you know, we've got feelers out in Taiwan as well, and I've an idea that it's one place where real difficulties are going to be put in our way.'

But his blue eyes gleamed with enthusiasm and Fee knew that he welcomed the challenge and would probably find his greatest satisfaction in securing a foothold in Taiwan, just because of the difficulties.

'Hong Kong has become too small for you, hasn't it?' she prompted, her previous resentment subsiding because, as always, she found herself drawn into and sharing his enthusiasm, as well as fascinated by his passion for property.

'Not in the sense that I'm bored or frustrated by what we've got here, and we'll continue to grow locally, but...' Simon thought a moment '...I'd just hate to ever find myself entirely satisfied.'

As a professional attitude, Fee could only respect it, but catching herself wondering whether he applied a similar creed to his personal life, or if the success of Rhodes Properties was a substitute for the permanency and growth so notoriously lacking in his relationships, she grew disturbed. Why did she have to be so interested in his private life, in danger of being intrigued—obsessed even?

Just then, a woman at the far side of the restaurant caught Simon's attention and he lifted a hand briefly in greeting. Fee was surprised. Although exceedingly glamorous, she was sure the woman must be approaching fifty.

Simon grinned, reading her thoughts.

'No, Fee, not an ex-lover, but an ex-stepmother... No, that's not accurate either. She married one of my favourite stepfathers after his marriage to my mother ended.'

Fee laughed. 'How do you ever remember who's who?'

Simon also laughed, but the sound had a dismissive ring. 'I don't, it's too complicated, but some of them kept in touch for a while. They were all nice people. Some of the women my father married or lived with even used to invite me to call them Mother, Mum, Mom, whatever... I obliged once or twice to begin with—my real mother didn't mind and they were as much part of my life as she was—but after a while it began to seem ridiculous because I realised it wasn't true, and that they'd be moving on in time.'

Fee shook her head. 'It's unbelievable!'

'It seemed normal to me,' Simon returned indifferently, 'although I could never understand why most of them got married so enthusiastically when they fell in love. That's what led to the only really troubled times, when whichever marriage it was broke up and there'd be shrieking matches over money, homes, cars—even a tank of tropical fish once, I remember!'

But it wouldn't have seemed normal to begin with, Fee reflected. Those people had taught him to believe it was normal. The very young boy would have felt disappointed when someone well-liked moved on, and her sensitive imagination supplied a picture of him growing older, learning to expect the disappointment, perhaps training himself not to feel it until, eventually, its absence was genuine because all the expectations he had left would be negative ones.

'I could never live like that,' she confided candidly.

Rejection hardened his face.

'I'm not asking you to, darling,' he drawled.

'No, I meant I couldn't have handled a childhood like yours,' she corrected him sharply.

'Yours was worse. At least I was never neglected,' he returned. 'But don't worry about it. It hasn't done me any harm.'

'That's debatable.' Fee's eyes sparkled with sudden anger.

'I've told you before, I am what I am on my own account, no one else's.'

Simon sounded irritable, the glitter in his eyes warning her that he was on the verge of losing his temper. Nervously, Fee pushed her glass further away from the edge of the table and then inadvertently caught his eye again. To her surprise, his angry expression was replaced by a sardonic smile, and she had to bite down hard and swallow an instinctive answering smile.

Horrible, superior, *knowing* man!

But at the same time she had to acknowledge that after all he did play fair—some of the time—because he could have used his past to appeal to her sympathy. Nor did she really believe he was devious, despite her earlier accusation, or at least not devious in the way that Mr Sheldon had been.

On the whole, though, she thought his openness probably stemmed quite simply from the fact that while he was interested in her at present—until someone else captured his attention—he didn't want her badly enough to go to any actual trouble over her, since manipulating her into one dinner date hardly constituted feverish pursuit.

'All right, I apologise.' She humoured him with an eloquent little smile. 'You're not much misunderstood, or more sinned against than sinning, or anything like that.'

'And as you see, I'm not totally unscrupulous either, Fee.' Temper in retreat, Simon was evincing a complex mixture of appreciation and complacency as he held her eyes. 'I've always tried to discourage women from casting me in that romantic role, although I've been too late in some cases—probably the Niobes you claim to have spent your life falling over.'

Fatally, she found herself liking him for the moment, a spontaneous smile curving her sensitive lips and dancing in her eyes.

'I was exaggerating about that,' she admitted demurely.

Simon was smiling back at her. 'Yes, I know.'

'Slightly,' Fee qualified pointedly, concerned that he might think she was flirting with him after that momentary softening.

He laughed and studied her in silence for several seconds.

'You don't want to dance again, do you? No,' he added drily as she began to shake her head. 'I didn't think you would. A liqueur?'

'No, thank you, I don't really like them.'

'Coffee, then?'

'No, but please may I try another of those little puddings while you have yours?'

They were miniature fantasies, all whirls and swirls of fine sugar and cream, and she had already enjoyed one while Simon had chosen the simplest fruit dish on the menu.

'You baby!' He had begun to grin, but a frown took over. 'You'll have me doing it too, just like Charles and Babs, thinking of you as the naïve teenager you used to be, if all your pleasures are so innocent. But you have grown up really, haven't you, Fee?'

She had tensed in response to the challenge, but she managed a serene smile.

'That teenager would have forced herself to swallow a liqueur because she thought it was the sophisticated thing to do,' she offered pointedly.

The last traces of Simon's frown vanished. 'Whereas the adult woman does exactly as she pleases. I'm glad to hear it. It's the only way to live.'

'Within reason,' she supplemented cautiously.

'Of course, and with due consideration for both other people and ourselves—and I suppose most of the women I go out with are really considering themselves by avoiding those concoctions like the plague. But I doubt if you'll ever have a weight problem—so please yourself while I please myself with some coffee, and then I'll take you home.' Seeing the wariness that crept into her dark blue eyes at this, Simon smiled ironically. 'Just that, Fee. As you know, I rarely make promises, but when I do I keep them, and a lot was implicit in that promise I made your mother hen of a sister earlier.'

But he never made the sort of big, important promises that changed lives or created happiness, she reflected with an odd sensation of sadness.

Simon kept his word, seeing her safely to the little flat, helping her sort out the unfamiliar keys and making sure she was locked in before departing.

'See you on Monday,' was all he said, and he had made no attempt to touch her.

So if he really felt any desire for her, it certainly wasn't the desperate, driving sort, Fee reflected tartly—unless he thought that by remaining somewhat elusive, playing hard to get in essence, he would pique a passionate response. But she couldn't really see him bothering with such subtle tactics. She wasn't important enough.

Then again, as Simon was known to be quite capable of losing interest long before a relationship got anywhere near the bedroom, maybe that was what was happening.

*　　*　　*

At work the following week, he made no reference to anything that had passed on the Saturday, and Fee found herself possessed by a lost, oddly uncertain feeling, frustrated by not knowing for sure if his impersonal attitude was dictated by the rules of their working relationship or was the simple result of loss of interest.

Whichever it was, she ought to be relieved, she reminded herself rather frantically, beginning to be frightened. She couldn't afford to start reacting emotionally to Simon. The fact that she reacted physically was bad enough, but she could deal with that—just as long as no personal emotion existed to weight physical attraction.

CHAPTER SEVEN

'I'LL need you with me, at least part of the time, and before we go I also want you to familiarise yourself with our various departments' methods sufficiently to be able to answer any questions from the Macau personnel while Freitas and I are busy or visiting our sites. Don't worry, he'll agree to your talking to them individually or in small groups, since you're uncomfortable with a lot of people looking at you. Thursday suits you, doesn't it?' Simon concluded.

'Yes, of course,' Fee responded composedly, trying not to be moved by his readiness to consider a personal foible. 'How do you want to get there? I suppose we'll need to make an early start?'

'Not horrendously early since we'll be staying overnight. Maynah Norman made hotel bookings some time ago, before she got it into her head to leave—haven't you come across some kind of confirmation yet? I decided we'd need part of Friday in which to cover what we don't fit in on Thursday, when we've got the official launch luncheon with all the obligatory speeches, and it's likely to overrun, especially with the Macau media in attendance as well as a few representatives from Hong Kong. Plus, I want to do something for Freitas on Thursday night—dinner, I think—just to welcome him on board as head of our Macau concern. I've invited him personally already—— What's wrong?' Simon digressed abruptly, finally noticing Fee's shuttered expression.

117

'Nothing.' But she sounded stilted, staring blankly at the screen on her desk for a moment before looking up at Simon, who had paused to issue his instructions on his way out to lunch with a banking tycoon. 'Will Maynah also have booked something for Thursday night, or should I go ahead and organise it?'

'Please. Get in touch with Freitas's assistant and see what she recommends if you're uncertain. For four of us, as there's a Senhora de Freitas.' Simon paused, impatience flickering in his eyes as they swept over her face. 'There *is* something wrong! Was it my mention of the media? I know a section gave you a bad time in Australia, but these will be business reporters and the like, Fee, and the only thing they're likely to sensationalise is the way we snatched Freitas.'

He was referring to an operation which had been carried out with a devastatingly efficient combination of hard and soft sell after the outside firm of head-hunters he had commissioned had recommended the man. Fee had only joined Rhodes Properties in the closing stages of the process, but she had heard about it and been impressed by the slightly ruthless way Simon had lured Senhor de Freitas into resigning from a high-powered position with excellent prospects in another property firm over in Macau.

Now she said stiffly, 'I know that. Nothing's wrong, Simon. You'd better go or you're going to be late for lunch.'

Still his eyes searched her face, and she could see the irritation tightening his features.

'I suppose it's something *personal*, and as usual you're adhering to the rules, which you'll accuse me of breaking if I insist on knowing what it is,' he suggested contemptuously.

'Nothing is——'

'Stop repeating that stupid word,' he interrupted shortly. 'Obviously *something* is worrying you, although if you had a date with Warren Bates for Thursday night or something of that sort maybe you're right and it's nothing important.'

It was Simon at his most cuttingly dismissive, and he departed without giving her a chance to retaliate.

She was being silly, Fee told herself. Just because one business trip had ended so disastrously, it didn't mean this one had to. Simon wasn't Vance Sheldon. She could trust Simon, even if he still had a whim about making her the next woman in his life—which seemed unlikely, given the aloofness that had characterised his recent behaviour until today's brief flash of temper.

She could trust him, and if she was going to let the idea of a business trip disturb her to this extent she should never have accepted this job, or any other like it, because such trips were inevitably part of the package.

Of course, she could have told Simon what was troubling her, but she had an idea that, instead of reassurance, such a confession would have elicited some of his most lacerating derision, and, while she was tougher than she had been in her teens and quite capable of answering back, she still wasn't as resilient as she would like to be where Simon was concerned. Somehow, he had the power to hurt and humiliate her. It wasn't that she thought he would take advantage of the vulnerability the confession would betray; she just shrank from the prospect of his scorn if he knew how stupidly trusting she had been.

So she kept telling herself that there was nothing to worry about—and she wasn't really worried, but the approaching trip to Macau had disinterred the memory of the one to Perth, and it haunted her mercilessly once more over the next couple of days.

The night before they left, she even woke trembling and wet with the perspiration of panic from a dream which was a replay of the fear followed by embarrassment that she had suffered in Perth.

She was unable to sleep again, and faint smudges marked the delicate skin beneath her eyes when she and Simon departed for Macau in the morning, Simon having elected to go by jet-foil, wanting the hour of time and the space it provided in order to go over some papers.

'Are you all right?' he demanded when he was satisfied, noticing her properly for the first time. 'The motion isn't making you feel sick, is it?'

Fee gave him a strained smile. 'No, I'm fine, thanks.'

'Have you been to Macau before?' The clever blue eyes were noting her pallor.

'Yes, once.' Her smile grew more natural. 'We spent a lovely day and evening there when Babs and I were children and my father and Angela were having one of their *rapprochements* and being all family-minded and responsible, so even Babs could relax and not have to worry about looking after herself and me.'

'Are you glad you came back to Hong Kong?'

'Yes, it's home. I loved Australia, but Hong Kong has got so much that's unique and special. I've been indulging myself since I got back, doing all my favourite things in all my best places, like shopping at Stanley Market and Mon Kok and even the night market.'

'Ah, a bargain-hunter,' he commented teasingly, still watching her face intently.

She laughed, grateful for the way he was keeping her mind from dwelling too much on the memory of Perth although they were breaking their rules by allowing the conversation to become personal.

'I got into the habit when Babs and I sometimes had to fend for ourselves when Angie was missing and we were afraid of running out of money before my father remembered to let us have some more. These days, though, it's a challenge—fun. With the salary I'm getting from Rhodes Properties, I could afford to shop in Nathan Road if I wanted to.'

'And you're happy with the job?' Simon's manner was oddly probing.

'Yes, of course, I've been very lucky and I'm grateful—to you and Charles.'

'Then why don't you relax?' He saw how her face tightened and laughed ironically. 'No, for some reason you can't, can you? And you've been especially tense these past few days——'

'I could relax if you stopped breaking the rules,' she asserted tautly, realising just how personal the conversation was now becoming.

'Then you're free to do so now, because we're about to arrive and it's back to business as usual,' he mentioned so coolly that she couldn't mistake the contemptuous rejection. 'I was merely filling a few idle minutes in a sociable way, darling, not trying to invade your mind or your space or whatever it is you're guarding so jealously.'

Fee was ashamed of herself, aware that she had overreacted, and she accepted the rebuke in silence, desperately trying to rationalise her tension out of existence. Clearly Simon was no longer interested in her as far as romantic or sexual dalliance went, so she had nothing to worry about.

Macau had a southern European atmosphere unique in Asia, despite the presence of Buddhist temples and such trees as banyans, and it was the ancient home of a happy blend of cultures.

The demands of the busy day that followed helped Fee immeasurably as she had no time to dwell on anything save what was required of her in her role as Simon's assistant, and in the evening the presence of Senhora de

Freitas provided a similar distraction. As so often happened, making the attraction of opposites more than a myth, the dynamic Senhor de Freitas had married the quietest of women whose painful shyness was exacerbated by her lack of fluency in English.

Shy herself, Fee could empathise, finding that the needs of such people, so much greater than her own, had the effect of helping conquer her own shyness, and once the *senhora* discovered that she adored children she relaxed properly, chattering unselfconsciously about her pre-school pair.

'I've always thought I'd also like to have two some day,' Fee mentioned at one stage and intercepted a cynical glance from Simon that made her skin prickle.

'You were kind to her,' he commented when the dinner party had broken up and they had returned to their hotel.

'You make it sound as if I was being patronising,' Fee flared indignantly as they entered a lift. 'If anyone was, it was you and Senhor de Freitas, looking on so indulgently whenever you paused in your superior, high-powered male conversation. She's sweet, and I know what it's like to be shy and feel horribly inadequate in company.'

'You, Fee? You could never be inadequate in any company!' He was openly sceptical and slightly flirtatious, eyes resting appreciatively on her straight, simple crimson dress for a moment before he grew more thoughtful. 'Although it's so recently that you *were* an agonisingly shy teenager that I suppose you do still remember.'

Right now, she felt just like that teenager again, shy and unequal to the expectations of sophisticated adults such as Simon, knowing she lacked the *savoir-faire* to behave like one herself in all but the least demanding situations, and desperately afraid of mistaking innocence for design—but even more terrified of making the opposite mistake.

It was all too familiar. She and Vance Sheldon had travelled up in a lift together like this, talking about the evening just behind them; and then the luxurious rooms Maynah Norman had booked months ago were next to each other here too, although separated by a good solid wall devoid of any doors. Fee had made very sure of that earlier.

The tension that was building up so relentlessly within her could no longer be contained when they reached her door and Simon moved her gently aside and took her key from her.

'No!' Wildly unthinking, she tried to push him out of the way again. 'You can't——'

'God, woman, what the hell is the matter with you now?' Simon demanded furiously, eyes blazing until he absorbed the horror in hers. 'Fee?'

She stared at him in appalled realisation, her eyes like bruises in her pale face. What was wrong with her? This was *Simon*——

'I'm sorry, I'm sorry, I know I'm over-reacting!' The words emerged punctuated by little gasping sighs. 'It's not you, Simon. It's just that everything keeps reminding me—the way you worked when we came over, and coming up in the lift, and the rooms—and I dreamt about it last night.'

'Reminding you of what?' His eyes held hers relentlessly.

'Of Mr Sheldon . . .' Her voice died away to a whisper and she was shaking.

'And the memory can do this to you? Do you still want——? But no, you were afraid!' Simon registered, adding almost urgently, 'What did Sheldon do to you, Fee?'

'In the end he didn't do anything.' Her little laugh was faint and brittle. 'He couldn't because I screamed and ran out of the room.'

Simon stared at her for a moment, absorbing it. Then he said firmly, 'And I'm not going to do anything to you either, but you're not going to have to scream or run way to prevent me, because I'm not going to touch you. I am coming in with you, though, because I want to know what happened and I'm not prepared to stand out here in the corridor while you tell me.'

Having made such a fool of herself, Fee wasn't prepared to compound it, and she allowed him to follow her in, turning to face him as he closed the door again.

'It was mostly my fault,' she vouchsafed bitterly.

'Tell me.'

Simon dealt in facts and, unlike nearly everyone else, he didn't instantly attempt to reassure her or insist on her innocence without giving her a chance to explain, something she found unexpectedly refreshing.

'The details are pretty much those that appeared in the Press except that the interpretation placed on them missed the truth. For instance, they thought what happened in Perth was the end of an affair after a screaming row in a hotel room, but Mr Sheldon had thought that night was going to be the *start* of an affair.' Pausing, Fee swallowed painfully. 'I was so stupid! He would invite his real assistant out socially several times a year, so when he asked me to the races I was pleased because I believed it meant he regarded me as part of the team. But I was his only guest and not even his wife or grown-up children were there. I was a bit uneasy because he kept touching me, but I didn't want to be like those women who read something lecherous into even the most innocent situations and I decided it was just because he was relaxing, away from the office, and drinking quite a lot of champagne. That's when the Press first got interested, wondering who I was, and apparently they started hinting about his having an affair right after that, but I don't read that kind of news usually, otherwise I might have started being suspicious, especially as he was taking much more notice of me at work, stopping to talk and asking me about my life away from the office... Then Miss Betancourt took some of her leave and there was this conference in Perth. I thought he'd go alone, but he asked me to accompany him and, like a fool, I was flattered, and hopeful, because I knew he had to approve of me if I was going to replace Miss Betancourt when she retired. He worked on the flight to Perth and when we arrived there was a gala dinner so I hardly had time to look at my hotel room, but when we got back— there was a communicating door to the next room and he came through almost at once...'

'It's all right, I can guess this bit,' Simon said expressionlessly as Fee paused, flushing, still missing most of her composure.

'Yes,' she confirmed gratefully. 'But he couldn't accept it, so I screamed as loudly as I could and he got such a shock that I was able to get away and out into the corridor. I think I was a bit hysterical because it's all mixed up in my mind now, but some reporters were hanging around; they'd recognised me from the race-meeting... He'd torn my dress and it was all over the papers the next day, but written up as a lovers' quarrel. Mr Sheldon was furious. He fired me that same night, right in front of all those reporters, and the hotel management found me another room—and then the next day he tried to take it back and make me go back to work for him... I couldn't! I did go to the office in Sydney one time when Miss Betancourt was back and she promised me he wouldn't be in that day, because she wanted to explain that I had the right to take some kind of action, but I didn't want the publicity it would bring. That day was horrible, though, I was nervous the whole time I was there...'

Fee's voice died away as she remembered the feeling, the confidence she had spent four years acquiring newly shattered, because she had been so wrong about so much, and her previous belief in her ability to take care of herself seemed like self-deception.

'And then he started phoning you?' Simon prompted, and Fee couldn't tell what he was thinking.

'Yes, because he wanted to restore his... his public standing. People were saying things, writing things to his discredit because he'd fired me so publicly, and even if it had been because I'd ended an affair, as they all thought, it was still viewed as unfair dismissal. It was awful in Australia.' She sighed shakily. 'There were always reporters; they'd found out where I lived and they'd all shout at me at once, trying to persuade me to tell my story. They even offered me money. Although he'd always been respected before, Mr Sheldon isn't popular, you see. When he started phoning, he wanted me to help him smooth it all over by going back to work as if nothing had happened; then people would start thinking it had all been a storm in a teacup, a real lovers' quarrel with lots of noise and no real content. I don't think he cared about my rejecting him so much as he did—does about the publicity. There were even cartoons. He blames me, of course, but also some of his rivals, other financiers and the like, for alerting the Press, setting him up, but I think it was simpler than that. He's a famous man and the public like to see famous people caught out, so they were probably after him purely in their own interests, but I think he has got a bit of a persecution complex.'

'How can you sound so understanding?' Simon suddenly exploded disgustedly. 'And the way you keep calling him *Mr* Sheldon, as if you still respected him! When he did that to you!'

'It's how I mostly thought of him,' Fee defended herself bleakly. 'He's fifty years old. That's why it never occurred to me that he might...that he might——'

'All men might, Fee,' Simon advised her harshly. 'God, you simply didn't think, did you? I've never heard of anyone so stupidly trusting.'

'Don't worry, I've learnt from the experience,' she asserted savagely, beginning to feel stronger now.

'Too well, judging by the way you over-reacted to my attempt to open the door for you just now.'

'I know, I told you, it was all just so similar——'

'The circumstances were entirely different,' he claimed arrogantly.

Fee saw the temper glinting in his eyes, but she was starting to feel angry again herself. Why had she told him so much, going into detail about the fool she had made of herself?

'I couldn't know for sure that they were,' she pointed out heatedly. 'Especially after some of the things you've said to me, even if you've changed your mind by now, and the way you manipulated me into going out to dinner with you that Saturday——'

'If you were so suspicious of me, why haven't you told me all this before?' Simon demanded. 'As a warning if nothing else, to let me know that you were on your guard?'

'Because I felt a fool!' she flared defiantly.

'I'm not surprised,' he conceded brutally, but then he seemed to relent slightly. 'All right, I'm not saying I might not have made a pass at you if I'd felt the impulse since this isn't strictly office hours——'

'Exactly! So you see——'

'But in no way am I like Vance Sheldon, Fee.'

Simon's voice was tight and hard, the words oddly jerky. With a shock, Fee realised that he was actually trying to control his temper; it was unexpected in a man as self-indulgent as he was, not usually given to bothering to restrain his impulses.

Inevitably, she began to feel contrite.

'Well, perhaps you aren't entirely,' she conceded in a breathless rush. 'Since at least you can control your temper——'

'Only with the greatest difficulty right this minute, darling,' he assured her sardonically.

'—although I still remember an occasion when you couldn't manage it,' Fee concluded, eyes darkening with the memory.

'You never will forget, will you? But do you really see me as a corrupt, conniving would-be seducer of reluctant women?' Simon pursued. 'Fee, I have never in my life attempted to force myself on an unwilling woman.'

'Since most of them are probably only too willing,' she quipped, disturbed by his increasing tension. 'And where one isn't, there are probably a hundred who are. All right, you're not like Mr Sheldon there, but probably only because he isn't really attractive to women. You are.'

With typical suddenness, all signs of temper vanished and he gave her a challenging glance. 'To you?'

Fee's eyes flashed in response to the flirtatious note. 'Simon——'

'All right, Fee.' Equally abruptly, he was serious, and she stiffened warily as he moved towards her. 'I'm well aware that the circumstances *are* actually too similar to those you experienced with Sheldon for you to be comfortable with me right now.'

'Don't,' she muttered as he lifted both hands to the sides of her face, his touch warm and light.

'I'm not,' he returned drily. 'I just want to make sure you know where you stand since obviously that's important to you. You stand exactly where you did before, your rules still apply to working hours if you insist and fall into abeyance out of them, but we'll call a moratorium on that side until we get back to Hong Kong, so you can sleep soundly and get rid of those shadows under your eyes. I won't be knocking on your door tonight. That's how far you can trust me. Goodnight.'

The brush of his lips across her brow was the lightest of touches, and yet she still felt it when he had gone, and she discovered that her trembling no longer had anything to do with stress. Instead it was the trembling of weakness and surrender.

He had told her how far she could trust him, but that wasn't very far—assuming he was still contemplating some sort of affair with her. He hadn't actually confirmed or denied it in so many words. If he wasn't, she had just made a colossal fool of herself.

'I thought you'd regret giving me the rest of the day off.' Fee was drily resigned, having just opened the door of her flat in response to Simon's knock. 'But ten o'clock on a Friday night, Simon?'

They had got back from Macau that afternoon. Characteristically, Simon had headed straight for the office, the only surprise his insistence that she go home.

He shook his head, laughing at her with his eyes.

'This is a social call.' Seeing the way her face closed defensively, he added lightly, 'Trust me, Fee.'

'Come in and have a drink, then,' she invited him with a cool little smile, allowing just a trace of reluctance to shade her voice. 'I was watching a movie.'

Acutely aware of how much vulnerability she had betrayed with her over-reaction the night before, she was determined to maintain her composure in his presence at all times in future, and not appear to be reading too much into his erratic personal interest.

Talking about work, he followed her into the kitchen and then the lounge, sitting down beside her on the couch from which she had been watching the movie on television. Unable to help herself, Fee stirred restlessly as he stretched out his long legs and leaned back in a relaxed attitude, one arm lying along the back of the couch behind her head.

She glanced at him and found his face turned towards her. He gave her a lazily intimate smile, suggestive of shared secrets.

'What's wrong?' he asked her idly.

'Nothing,' Fee lied irritably and returned her gaze determinedly to the television screen.

Simon watched for a minute too before saying, 'I've seen this before. It's not bad.'

'Don't tell me what happens!' she urged quickly.

She had been about to offer to switch it off, but if he had seen it before perhaps he would get bored and leave.

Simon laughed softly. 'I'll never spoil anything for you, sweetheart ... No sign of Warren Bates, even on a Friday night?'

'He did ask me out, but I said no.'

Fee wasn't sure what had prompted her to tell him that. She only knew that his presence, along with his casual attitude, was filling her with an odd churning resentment.

After several phone calls from Warren, she had discovered sadly that they had very little to talk about, partly because he tended to lecture, eschewing the give and take of normal conversation, and she knew she wouldn't enjoy an evening out in his rather jumpily uptight company.

Simon looked mildly curious, but almost immediately another deeply complex expression crossed his face, before ordinary complacency finally replaced it.

'Because I'm the only man you want?'

Rigid with tension, Fee sensed the slight movement of the arm behind her just before she felt a light hand against her head, fingers twining in her loose shining curls. He was too near; not only his hand but the warmth of him seemed to reach out and touch her, and she was also aware of the pleasant scent of his aftershave.

'You said I could trust you,' she protested tightly, her resolve never to over-react again instantly forgotten.

Simon was utterly unabashed, although he did drop his hand to the back of the couch after a few seconds. 'You can. Relax, sweetheart.'

But she couldn't, and nor could she look at Simon, but lowering her eyes made her feel even more disturbed as she saw the rapid way in which her breasts rose and fell beneath the black T-shirt she was wearing with her jeans.

She had lost track of the film's plot, but she pretended to be absorbed and Simon sat quietly beside her, apparently engrossed. Fee couldn't concentrate, acutely conscious of him sitting so shamelessly close to her, touching her hair every so often and smiling occasionally if she risked a glance at him. Those smiles disturbed her even more; they were so warmly intimate, the accompanying gleam in his eyes promising all sorts of erotic delights.

Once he dropped his arm from the back of the couch to Fee's shoulders, pulling her close in a single swift movement.

'There's something about sitting primly side by side on a couch instead of stretched out horizontally that reminds me of my earliest teenage romancing,' he murmured outrageously into her ear.

For a weak moment, Fee knew an urge to lean against him as his warm breath drifted across her cheek. He was so strong, so hard that she felt sheltered and safe held there in the curve of his arm, and yet wildly excited at the same time, her body stirring inwardly, her heart thundering. Her head was drooping, seeking the comfort of his shoulder, before she found the strength to jerk away.

'Can you really remember that far back?' she demanded with mock-incredulity, but he only laughed.

'I spoke to Charles earlier,' he mentioned after watching the television screen for a minute or two. 'He says there has been just one further call from Sheldon since the one you took that time I was at the house... What's wrong?'

Simon frowned as he observed the spark of anger that had appeared in Fee's eyes.

'I didn't know,' she said tautly, her face suddenly shadowed.

'Because you weren't told? Those people!' Simon exploded furiously, making Fee jump. 'I'm going to tell them—make sure they accept it once and for all! You're not a baby, and you'd feel a damned sight better about it all if you knew the score instead of being kept in the dark, just because they're convinced you need protecting.'

'Don't interfere!' Fee snapped. 'Why were you talking to Charles about it anyway? You're as bad as them. If I've got problems in my life, I'll deal with them myself. I don't need them to look after me, and I don't need you, so stay out of it.'

'Oh, yes, you coped with Sheldon so effectively, didn't you, letting yourself in for all that distress?' he taunted. 'But I am not sheltering you, Fee. I'm telling you there was a call. Apparently Babs took it. She said he sounded drunk, and demanded your return, but he rang off when he realised she wasn't you.'

'Yes, he does drink.' Fee controlled her resentment. 'Not regularly, but when he does I've heard it's a real binge, and it would have been getting on in the evening in Sydney that first time he rang here.'

'At least there's little chance of his discovering your number here, and he doesn't know where you're working... I shouldn't have given him my name that time I spoke to him, but let's hope he doesn't make the connection. It could cause problems for our switch-board—— Yes, I know you can take care of yourself, but as an employee you come under my protection and have a right to expect it, at least while you're at work.'

'Thank you.' Fee accepted it as gracefully as she could.

It helped to talk openly about Vance Sheldon, she dis-covered, and it helped even more to hear Simon making fun of him. The haunted look left her eyes, and she even giggled a little as he became more colourfully slanderous.

He left when the film ended, touching Fee lightly on the cheek before standing up.

'You see, Fee, you can trust me,' he said casually. 'Sleep well.'

But Fee didn't think she would.

Was he interested in her—whether still interested, or interested again—or was he merely being the concerned, caring employer she knew him to be?

At work on Monday, Simon made no reference either to what had been said between them in Macau or to the Friday evening, and Fee deliberately kept her manner equally impersonal, despite her resentment, knowing full well that he was capable of losing interest in her between one day and the next, and half convinced that it had already happened, though his silence could just be Simon's way of keeping the rules that applied to their working relationship.

That remained unchanged, increasing the respect she felt for Simon as her boss, despite his occasional impatience, and the odd explosion of temper, although so far she had mercifully escaped being a recipient of his most blistering criticism.

The first time she made a serious mistake that was a result of her own carelessness rather than lack of familiarity with the job or Simon's failure to explain, he came stalking into her office and placed the offending document in her hands in ominous silence. The error was so stupid and so obvious that she was ashamed.

'Oh, Simon, I'm so sorry!' she apologised in distress. 'How could I be so stupid?'

A tightness around his mouth and a stormy look in the blue eyes usually heralded a short, spectacular explosion of temper, and Fee braced herself for a scorching confirmation as to her stupidity, but to her surprise it didn't come. Simon stood there looking down at her flushed face and the apprehension turning her dark blue eyes almost black, and she saw him relax slowly.

'It's all right, don't be upset. Just do it over again,' he said, and paused, following it with an irritable shrug. 'And why aren't I bawling you out? Hell, it must be catching, this business of not wanting to upset you that makes your family try to keep you wrapped in cotton wool... In one of your most usual, rather tart moods, you could take it and probably yell back at me, but when you look at me like that and sound so contrite I know I'd feel like a bully if I shouted at you!'

Fee smiled shakily. 'I'd deserve it this time.'

He shook his head absently, lost in thought for several seconds. She was still seated, but turned away from her desk, Simon standing beside her, and she didn't think he was consciously aware of his hand dropping to rest over her shoulder.

'I've begun to see the old, teenage Fee quite often lately,' he mused finally, still thoughtful. 'I missed her to begin with, when you first came home, but there's still a little of her in there, isn't there? It's funny, I've always thought of myself as being attracted to extroverts... Why do you look tired?'

'I'm fine,' Fee protested quickly.

She suddenly felt acutely vulnerable, terrified of his guessing just how much of her new persona was mere façade, although she wasn't sure why the prospect frightened her. He could hardly take advantage of it if she remained on her guard.

The answer to his question was that she was sleeping badly, afflicted by a strange, tormenting restlessness. It was because she hadn't really settled down yet and was still adjusting to being back in Hong Kong and having a new job, she had to assume. She could go to bed and lie there, with her mind going over and over the day she had just spent, but instead of lulling her such thoughts just made her feel more wide awake and restless than ever. Oh, and, if she was honest, she was finding working for Simon increasingly disturbing—exciting too, but definitely disturbing, making her suspect herself of the ultimate folly—except that it couldn't possibly be true. She couldn't be falling in love with him. She knew too much about him and she had too much regard for her heart; she wanted it to stay whole, and Simon broke hearts.

Fee turned her head slightly, her gaze coming to rest obliquely on the lean, tanned hand curved over her shoulder, and she had to fight an urge to let her lips drop to its capable strength and kiss the darkly golden skin.

Oh, God, what was she thinking of? She lifted helpless eyes to Simon's face and he gave her a rather twisted smile.

'No, I'm not supposed to touch you at work, am I?' he remembered sardonically, removing his hand. 'But where else can I? Don't worry, sweetheart, it doesn't mean anything.'

'It doesn't matter,' she muttered, struggling to quell an inner agitation.

Simon looked oddly arrested for a moment, scrutinising her face intently and finally producing a complacent smile.

'Get that done again,' he reminded her with a gesture, and departed abruptly.

What had she done? That smile of his worried her. He must have sensed that weak moment of hers, but it had only happened because she was tired, and vulnerably off guard in her relief at having been spared a caustic diatribe. He would soon realise that it hadn't been something he could build on—as long as she was careful. She wished he weren't so attractive, though.

CHAPTER EIGHT

AFTER taking a call from Senhor de Freitas the following Friday afternoon, Simon requested Fee's presence in his office.

'Those figures for Macau—can I leave it to you to get them finished today?' he asked with the confidence that always bolstered her own belief in herself. 'I have to get out to the New Territories and the time it's going to take me to sort this problem out means I probably won't be coming back here today as I'm going out this evening, but Freitas happens to be coming over to Hong Kong tomorrow, so I'd like to take the opportunity to go over the figures with him personally. I've told him to come up to my place on the Peak as it's Saturday.'

'Then if you're not coming back to the office again today, I'd better deliver them to you at home tomorrow,' Fee suggested, hating herself for wondering what he would be doing and with whom that night.

'Would you?' As he considered her offer, a fleeting look of curiosity crossed his face. 'If it's not one of your particularly sacred Saturdays... How will you get there, taxi or tram?'

'I've got my own car now,' she admitted with some pride. 'I got excellent repayment terms on the strength of this job. Charles helped me choose it.'

'You should have asked me. I know much more about cars than he does,' Simon claimed arrogantly.

'Oh, you know more about everything than anyone,' Fee retorted, forgetting their rules for once, riled by his assumption that she might turn to him for anything.

'Thank you,' he returned blandly, a gleam in his eyes. 'Well, don't come too early. Freitas said he'd aim for twelve, but we'll have other business to talk about anyway, so it doesn't matter if you're a bit late. He's coming alone, but why don't you have lunch with us? That reminds me, please ring Mrs Deng and let her know—two or three, just as you please, and even if you don't please I still don't want you pitching up at the crack of dawn, because I'm attending one of those fund-raising affairs for the refugee camps tonight and they always go on until late. Are you going?'

'No, but I think Charles and Babs are.'

'Come with me?' Simon invited her, smiling ironically as she started shaking her head. 'No, you wouldn't, would you? What are you doing?'

'If I finish the work you want in time, I'll probably look in on tonight's battle of the bands. I saw one of the groups in Australia and they're really good.'

'Is Warren Bates going with you?'

'No...' Something in his expression disconcerted her, and she added quickly, 'Shouldn't you be on your way?'

'Hell, yes!' Simon glanced at his watch, characteristically losing interest in the conversation as his mind flew ahead to a sensitive maintenance problem that had developed at one of his major properties in the industrially developed New Territories and with which he wanted to deal personally. 'All right, leave everything else and get those figures done. See you tomorrow.'

As a teenager, Fee had never been included in invitations to Simon's parties, so she had only ever seen his house from the outside.

She had to identify herself before a man who was presumably Mr Deng would let her drive through the gates at eleven forty-five the following morning. He indicated a tiled circle at the top of the short, steep drive and after parking her Honda Ballade she got out and gazed up at the unusual house. It was a modern building, apparently a series of interlocked boxes on different levels, although she couldn't work out how the effect had been achieved or imagine what the interior must be like; yet there was nothing stark about it and its colour, a pale pink wash, was the last she would have expected Simon to choose. Where the roofing was visible she could see that the tiles too were pink, but a deeper, warmer shade, and Mr Deng must have green fingers because marvellous cascades of creepers and shrubbery softened the effect still further.

The heavy panelled front door—Thai or Burmese teak, she thought—was closed, but as she approached the steps leading up to it Simon appeared from one side of the house, swiftly descending another short flight of steps.

'Fee!' he welcomed her. 'Come round.'

Fee couldn't say a word for the moment. He was wearing nothing but a pair of swimming-trunks which had obviously once been brightly multi-coloured but were now faded to soft, almost pastel shades, and the sight of all that beautiful golden flesh on display was just too much for her senses.

She swallowed, discovering that her mouth had gone dry. Realising she was staring, she hastily averted her eyes.

'Here,' she offered tautly, thrusting the folder she was carrying at him. 'I must go.'

'No, you mustn't,' Simon contradicted her, taking her arm. 'Come and admire my pool. I should have told you to bring a bikini. There are probably a few lying around but no one I know is quite your size and shape... You look nice. I was wrong about mini-skirts. These long skirts you sometimes wear suit you; but why do you always wear those straight, severe things for the office?'

'Miss Betancourt's training,' she murmured, recovering and letting him guide her up the steps, although she wished he would take his hand away.

It was another hot day, slightly hazy, and the swimming-pool sparkled at the centre of an unusual surrounding deck, plain square tiles irregularly interspersed with subtly patterned ones. At one end a moulded oval garden table was protected by a sunshade, also oval, with a few chairs and sun-loungers close by, their cushions matching the sunshade. Releasing her, Simon put the folder down on the table and turned to look at Fee with a blazing smile, not saying a word as his eyes travelled over her face in its frame of casual curls and on to the slenderness of her figure, in a way that almost convinced her that he could actually see what lay beneath the subtle violet material of her sleeveless top and the folds of her informal violet and soft crimson skirt. She looked back at him helplessly, locked into a terrifying vulnerability, because something had changed and this wasn't the Simon of the office.

'It makes a tantalising change to have you to myself away from the office. Such a rare occasion calls for a celebration of some kind,' he told her softly, still smiling, but rather quirkily now as he continued with lazy humour, 'I was actually planning to be incredibly nice and hospitable, to let you relax and entertain you with my wit and charm, at least to begin with... But I don't think I really want to wait, do you? Come here, darling.'

But Fee couldn't move, so he came to her.

She was trembling violently, filled with a hot, sweet excitement as Simon drew her into his arms, and she offered him her lips quite instinctively.

His mouth moved so gently over hers, and in it, that she felt as if she were dissolving, and a shaken sigh escaped her as he ended the kiss. She had dropped her keys without realising it, and her hands had been pressed against his chest, but now she slid her arms round him. His back was warm from the sun and her fingers stirred languidly against the firm flesh, loving the smoothness of his skin.

'That's nice,' Simon murmured and she felt his slight ripple of response. 'I don't think I've ever known anyone quite as lovely as you. You have such a beautiful mouth...'

He claimed it again, and several times more, but never lingering too long, those tenderly erotic kisses interspersed with others lightly skimming her delicate jawline, brushing her cheeks, straying to her throat and nuzzling at the fair, polished skin beneath her ears. Only when it was Fee, hopelessly adrift on a sweeping tide of longing, who clung and drew him insistently in again when he would have released her mouth once more did Simon cease those teasing interludes, his kisses growing intensely intimate, gently possessive and finally passionately sensual.

Fee's breathing was ragged as he lowered her to one of the cushioned sun-loungers, half in sun, half in shade.

'Simon,' she whispered wonderingly, lifting shaking fingers to the taut, intent face just above hers.

He was so beautiful, a golden idol in the sun, then mysteriously shadowed as he moved into the shade in which she lay. Then her eyes adjusted to the change and she saw that he was smiling at her as she traced the tense line of his cheek.

'I love the way you touch me,' he confessed. 'So gently that it makes me want to do the same for you...'

He bent to her, half lifting her so that he could cradle her in his arms, and Fee had never felt so wanted, so cherished, so feminine. He was kissing her again and she was responding with a wantonness that was both wild and tender, while her hands roamed caressingly over his flesh in their own act of adoration.

Her top buttoned up the front but she was unaware of his unfastening it until he came to the clip of her plain white bra, skilfully freeing her small firm breasts. Then he drew back a little, suddenly very still as his eyes came to rest on the pale pearly sheen of the gently sloping mounds, their erect peaks the same beautiful colour as the natural flush of her mouth.

'Fee?' he prompted questioningly on an odd, urgent note.

He touched her as if he was reaching out to discover something sacred and long-dreamed of, tracing the curve of her breasts, and circling them so tenderly that Fee was choked by a hot rush of emotion.

His mouth dropped to hers again as one arm drew her in, close and tight now, and a hand still cupped one breast from beneath, fingers rhythmically massaging at her flesh, which seemed to swell to fill the shape of his hand.

Simon's mouth was passionate now, insistently demanding, and as Fee wound her arms about his neck a hand lifted to his bright head, she felt him shudder slightly with sensation and she herself was suddenly frantic in his embrace, not knowing what she herself truly wanted—less or more, an end or continuation—but wanting what he wanted, because he was *Simon*.

As he raised his head, her agitated, strangled gasp made him stiffen momentarily and then, unbelievably, he was relaxing and withdrawing from her embrace, quickly refastening her bra and smiling at her.

'Enough for now? It's all right, sweetheart, we've got all day and, to be honest, I hadn't intended things to get quite so out of hand right here and now, but you are so very lovely.' His voice had been reassuring, but amusement laced it as he added, 'Only, please button that top, or plans and intentions aren't going to count for much.'

What had she been doing? As the shock of reality hit her, Fee flushed, fumbling awkwardly to obey his re-

quest, her vision blurring as she tried to focus on re-
calcitrant buttons.

'I should have known!' But she was still too agitated
to make the attack coherent initially, and furious with
this man who could make her forget all the things she
really wanted and seduce her into believing instead that
she wanted him and the superficial short-term affair he
was offering her. 'You appear to be forgetting that I'm
here on a work-related matter, Simon, so this counts as
office hours. But, if you don't mind, I won't wait to see
Senhor de Freitas. You don't really need me, do you?'

'You're staying for lunch.' Simon had stood up.

'No! I wasn't going to anyway,' Fee asserted sharply.
'I told Mrs Deng lunch for two when I rang her for you
yesterday.'

'Yes, two. You and me, Fee,' Simon elaborated. 'No
one will disturb us at all today.'

'What about Senhor de Freitas?' She indicated the
folder lying on the table as she got to her feet. 'He should
be here any minute.'

'Oh, he cancelled our appointment early this morning.
Apparently his two infants woke up with spots and raging
temperatures, and as our meeting wasn't urgent and it
is the weekend he felt he should stay home and help his
wife with them,' Simon announced blandly, following it
with an idly reflective smile. 'Usually that sort of thing
annoys me. People shouldn't get married; they're always
wanting to change appointments or take time off to tend
sick spouses or children, or because of anniversaries,
birthdays, babies being born and what-have-you... But
this time I wasn't complaining.'

Fee's head had jerked upwards, her flush fading,
leaving her face so dead white that her eyes looked black.
Her mouth shook momentarily, and then it tightened.

'Again,' she realised flatly. 'Like Mr Sheldon.'

Simon's features tautened slightly, but then a glint of amusement appeared in his vivid eyes.

'You weren't exactly screaming for help, darling,' he drawled.

Fee was shaking her head vehemently, aware of a wound in her heart, as if someone had just stabbed her. Simon.

'You set me up,' she accused tightly. 'You let me come up here when you could quite easily have rung and told me you wouldn't be needing those figures today after all.'

'And miss out on our...celebration?' Simon prompted, the gentle, indolent mockery incensing her still further. 'These aren't working hours, so the rules don't apply. There's no work to be done, so let's play, I reasoned. We both deserve to after the work we've put in, getting the Macau project launched, don't you think?'

'Oh, this was supposed to be my reward, was it?' she urged savagely. 'Getting to see the great Simon Rhodes half naked, being kissed by him——'

'And kissing him back very satisfactorily,' he pointed out, beginning to laugh. 'So it was my reward as well, and our private celebration. I've enjoyed the anticipation of it too, although I'm a little surprised at how long I spun it out... Do you know, I haven't made love to any other woman since before that party when you'd just come home? Hell, maybe I've really reformed after all. *You've* reformed me, Fee!'

He sounded so delighted with the idea which had clearly only just occurred to him that, in other circumstances, Fee might have laughed, but his continuing refusal to take her anger seriously outraged her, and her eyes blazed.

'Reform, Simon?' she prompted, bitingly sceptical. 'I'd have said the reverse, because this—today—is absolutely typical of you, isn't it? I suppose I should have guessed, but I honestly believed you'd never really behave like Mr Sheldon. But you have—just like him!'

'You didn't want him, while you know you do want me.' Still frustratingly unperturbed by her rage, Simon was smiling lazily at her, and the arrogant taunt contained an almost tender note that seemed to mock her, heightening her resentment.

'Get this, Simon—I do not want a liar, someone who takes advantage of me. I trusted you to be open about things!' She was so enraged that it was stealing her breath, and she had to stop, coincidentally spotting her keys and snatching them up.

'But then you do tend to trust too much, don't you? Didn't your experience with Sheldon teach you anything?' he mocked gently. 'I did warn you just how far you could trust me. Never trust anyone completely, darling. We're all thinking only of ourselves——'

'Shut up!' She didn't want to hear him admitting to these things; she didn't want them to be true—not of Simon. 'Oh, yes, I know I was stupid, but that doesn't make what you did any better.'

'Oh, was there room for improvement? I don't usually get complaints, but come here and let's—celebrate a little more, and see if I can do better.'

'Celebrate what?' Fee was caustic. 'My being a fool or your being—what you are? And that's something I despise!'

'Don't you think you're over-reacting slightly?' Simon enquired with sardonic interest, still essentially untroubled although his expression had hardened. 'You're starting to bore me, Fee.'

'I would have eventually anyway,' she flared. 'That's axiomatic, isn't it? If a woman interests Simon Rhodes to begin with, she bores him in the end—because there has to be an end. This happens to be ours.'

'Oh, sweetheart, this is only the beginning,' he retorted, still indolently confident, real enjoyment sparkling in the blue eyes. 'Although I'll accept the postponement of our celebration since in your present mood you're likely to rip me to shreds if we get close again. But why don't you stay for lunch anyway?'

He really was enjoying himself, Fee realised furiously—and she was providing the enjoyment, actually entertaining him by being so angry and showing it, dignifying his duplicity by reacting to it instead of walking out of here. Not any more, though.

'No!'

Her answer was violent and she swallowed everything else she might have said, turning and walking away, resisting the temptation to halt and let him have it after all, although the soft laughter that followed her tried her sorely.

She was still furious when she reached her apartment, but it couldn't last. The anger was a defence, and the reality from which it shielded her was too powerful to be denied any longer. At least it had carried her safely home, though, so the worst, first throes of her descent into sheer misery were mercifully private. Simon's cynical manipulation and total absence of repentance had angered her; but more than that they had hurt, and she couldn't bear it, so here she was, crying over him.

Just like all the others, she reflected bitterly, hopelessly in love and heartbroken.

Disliking him, resenting him, for all sorts of reasons and on behalf of so many people including herself, had been such a habit; otherwise she would have known long ago—oh, and hadn't she suspected the truth lately, and then complacently convinced herself that she wasn't that stupid?—because she thought she had loved him a long time and had perhaps even sensed her capacity to do so all those years ago when she had been so self-consciously awkward under his eyes, and so devastated by the public humiliation he had caused her when she had spilt her drink over him and ended up in his lap.

She had been a child then and her family, or Babs at any rate, still treated her as if she were one, probably because she had never challenged their perception of her with any real conviction—because some subconscious, self-protective part of her had wanted her to remain a child, safe from loving Simon? Children didn't fall in love with Simon Rhodes. Women did. But she *was* a woman and it had been inevitable, the fight always futile. Most women fell in love with him; a few of them got over it.

Fee didn't believe she ever would.

She was subdued all weekend, too deep in despair to spend more than odd moments wondering if their usual rules would still be in force when she went to the office on Monday, or if her emotional reaction to his duplicity would have caused Simon to lose interest in her at last, once he stopped being amused by it, especially as even in the midst of that amusement he had claimed that she was beginning to bore him.

On Sunday, eager to try out her built-in barbecue, she invited Babs and Charles over for lunch, but her mood and the fact that the day suddenly turned grey and damp made the occasion less than a lively success.

'Oh, baby, what's wrong?' Babs took the opportunity to demand anxiously when the two of them went inside, leaving Charles to make sure the fire was truly out. 'You're so quiet. Are you lonely here all on your own, or is something wrong at work?'

'*Work* is fine. Simon——'

The slight inadvertent emphasis plus her inability to get Simon's name out properly made Babs's eyes widen in realisation.

'Oh, no, Fee, not you? Not Simon!'

'Why not?' Fee returned bleakly. 'It happens to nearly everyone else. Why not me?'

'But...*he's* not actually interested in *you*, is he?' Babs was suddenly suspicious.

'Oh, only in his usual casual way,' Fee offered dismissively. 'It will pass. We all know that.'

'Have you——?'

'No!' Fee cut in. 'You know me, Babs. I don't want the things he enjoys...affairs. I want to get married, and be loved, and know my husband is as faithful as I am, and have children; those things.'

'Yes, of course you do. You mustn't give in to him, Fee,' Babs advised rather dramatically. 'He'll break your heart. You have to resist him!'

Fee tried to laugh, and shivered, suddenly chilled.

'When he's irresistible? I'm not sure if I can go on doing it, Babs, but he has had so many lovers, and hurt them, even if he didn't mean to. I don't want to end up like them, but I'm so scared I will.'

Babs put a comforting arm round her. 'He's a swine.'

'It's starting to rain.' Charles joined them.

'Do you know what that friend of yours has done to poor little Fee?' Babs challenged furiously. 'Simon Rhodes. You must pack that job in, Fee—Charles, you have to speak to him. In fact, I'm going to——'

'Cut it out, Babs,' Charles roared, making them both jump. 'Just stay out of it! It's their business. They're both adults, and if you stopped treating Fee like a baby and worrying about her all the time, trying to improve on the job you did when she really was in need of mothering, maybe you wouldn't have such a hang-up about having some real babies of your own.'

'I've told you I'm no good——'

Suddenly they were both yelling at each other, but then Charles stopped and said, 'We're leaving—now! Sorry about this, Fee, and thanks for lunch. It was great.'

Fee hated quarrels at the best of times so she let them go without protesting. Their conflict was more than she could bear just then, added to the weight of her personal distress over Simon, and especially as it seemed that she was indirectly responsible for a marital problem she hadn't even guessed existed.

Her heart sank when she heard a knock at the door only a few minutes after their departure. Babs must have refused to get into the car with Charles——

But Simon stood at the door, ironic impatience flickering in his eyes as he observed her pale, tense face.

'Don't tell me yesterday is still bothering you,' he began sardonically, but then he gave her a more searching glance. 'No, it's not that, is it? Something has upset you. Something to do with Sheldon? Or—I passed Charles and Babs driving away. What's the trouble?'

Fee hesitated, beginning to tremble. Part of her was frantic, desperate to get away from him and the pain of loving him and knowing she could never have him, which was unbearably heightened by the simple fact of his presence. But in her vulnerable state Simon's question sounded like an offer of comfort, admittedly too impatient to constitute caring or concern, but nevertheless a reaching out of sorts.

'Babs and Charles . . . they were fighting and I think it might be my fault,' she confided through chattering teeth as he stepped inside and closed the door. 'I didn't know before . . . She doesn't want to have babies and Charles does, and I know it must be because she believes she'll be no good as a mother because she still feels guilty about how she sometimes failed me, but she was only a child——'

'That's enough,' Simon stopped her tautly as a gasping sob convulsed her, a single stride bringing him to her, his hands going to her upper arms which were clammy beneath the short sleeves of the black T-shirt she was wearing with jeans. 'You're frozen... Your bloody family. Here, put this on.'

He was shrugging out of the casual biker's jacket he had on and wrapping it round her. Fee shivered violently.

'Simon, I don't want to——' she began agitatedly.

'It's all right, I'm just here to *talk*, Fee, and anything else is up to you. Forget Charles and Babs and their problems, and let's concentrate on ours. Listen to me,' Simon added quietly but emphatically, pulling her close for a moment. 'Whatever the trouble is, it's their responsibility, not yours, and worrying about it or feeling guilty isn't going to help anyone. You are not to blame for any neuroses or hang-ups Barbara may have, because they're hers; she created them.'

'That's one of your favourite theories, isn't it?' she prompted tartly, finally beginning to gain some control over her distress. 'That's why you won't blame your parents and all their partners for the way you are.'

Simon gave a faint grin. 'I don't consider that the "way I am" constitutes a hang-up, but you're right. I'll go so far as to admit that the way they lived may have *affected* me, as I think you once put it, but they're not to blame for anything, because being affected—I refuse to say influenced—is a voluntary act; we let ourselves be affected... But I didn't come here to discuss those people. I want to talk about us, and the rest is up to you. No hidden agenda this time, Fee, because I'd like to have your trust back, please.'

Still distraught, Fee half accepted it, almost welcoming the way he was taking charge—taking over!—relaxing slightly and her teeth ceasing to chatter.

'I'm sorry, I know I'm being boring and probably *over-reacting* again,' she acknowledged acidly. 'It's just that Babs is so special. It makes me feel cold, wondering what would have become of me if I hadn't had her when my father and Angela forgot about us, because I was even littler than she was and couldn't do a thing for myself in the beginning.'

'I know; it almost makes her general silliness forgivable,' Simon conceded, shaking his head slightly. 'What a childhood, and what a paradox too, because, while you were utterly neglected in most practical ways, you obviously never lacked for love, and only occasionally for money, which most people regard as the two most important things in life... But stop worrying about Babs. You're not responsible for her limitations, whether real or imagined.'

'I know. Oh, it's just that everything seems to have come at once, all in one weekend,' Fee excused her distress, with no thought of trying to minimise her reaction to the previous day's events or pretending that she had dismissed his behaviour.

'You're too emotional for your own good. That was also a very emotional reaction yesterday, wasn't it?' Simon added, glancing at her pale face. 'Not that I didn't enjoy it all, but after you'd gone I started wondering if I should have taken it a bit more seriously. Plus, I regretted losing your trust—because I knew you'd been starting to trust me, and I'd taken advantage of it. But hell, Fee, you do want me.'

A wan smile crossed her face, because it was so typical of Simon. Sharing none of the idealism that made an affair so impossible for her, he saw that as the only thing that mattered, everything else being extraneous.

'Yes.' There was no point in denying it.

He slanted her a quick smile. '*Yes*, so there's no need for me to take short-cuts without warning you. I'd like you to trust me again, so from now on I mean to be open about the whole thing. I'd like to have an affair with you, and I hope you'll let me stay with you tonight, or come home with me, but if you don't feel ready yet then I can wait, and not try to con you, or exploit you in any way.'

Swallowing painfully, Fee shook her head.

She could never have an affair with him. Ideals apart, she loved him too much, and she knew she lacked the emotional resilience to be able to bear it when he tired of her, as he inevitably must. She simply didn't have the temperament to take what he was offering philosophically and accept that she must pay for it with a certain amount of suffering afterwards, as other easygoing or perhaps just plain reckless women seemed able to do.

Or maybe they simply couldn't help themselves. Glancing at him, and feeling her heart wrenched by love, Fee suddenly wasn't sure if she could help herself either—only how could she happily have an affair with him, knowing all the time that it must end? I would destroy her. Oh, she had to stay strong!

Simon followed her into the lounge, accepting a glass of the red wine she and the others had been drinking with lunch.

He came and sat beside her on the couch and she tensed.

'So let's talk about all these complications we have to get out of the way,' he suggested drily, sitting turned towards her.

Fee moved her head in denial, saying sharply, 'There's no point, nothing to talk about. Once and for all, Simon, I can't—I just cannot have an affair with you.'

'Can I remind you that you want to?' he asked softly and moved, dropping a quick warm kiss on her lips before sitting back again, a hand lifted to her face, fingers trailing lightly down the side of her cheek and over the satiny smoothness of her slender neck. 'But I suppose I have to accept that it's not as simple for you as it is for me, so let's hear what the difficulties are.'

A quivering sigh escaped her, and she stirred languidly. Most of the difficulties seemed absurdly irrelevant suddenly, but on another level she knew that they were real—only how could she go on resisting him, when he was making her feel like this, so warm and weak, trembling inwardly and outwardly? Perhaps if she explained her problem properly he would understand and—perhaps the problem would turn out to be something he could banish for her. The thought turned itself into a fatal wish, and, realising it, she stiffened, furious with herself.

'There isn't any one specific thing, just all your other lovers generally,' she snapped, and saw him smile. 'All right, I know it must seem hilarious to you with all your experience, and I suppose if I had a bit more of my own—I mean, if I'd had several affairs myself—I'd be able to see other people's affairs in some sort of perspective, and be used to not letting them matter as long as they were over and done with, and maybe most of yours wouldn't matter... But I am not used to it, Simon!'

'Never mind my past for a moment. What about yours?' Simon sounded slightly amused. 'You've got me intrigued. Just how few affairs have you had, since the Sheldon business wasn't one, as I believed? I've realised since you told me what really happened there that you've retained a degree of innocence, but I hardly imagined you regarded your limited experience as some sort of handicap, especially when you're so scathing of my... wealth of it, shall we say? How innocent are you really?'

His fingertips still stroked lightly at the tender curve of her throat and it took a moment or two to concentrate on the question.

'When I've spent all my life among people who go in for lots of affairs, starting with Angela, and then people like you, I'm not likely to have much mental innocence left, am I?' she prompted with a wry little grimace. 'But in myself—practically, I mean...well, it's total really.'

Simon looked so shocked that she blushed. Suddenly he was no longer touching her, and the blue eyes were narrowed with suspicion as they raked her face.

'Total? What about Warren Bates?' he demanded.

Fee shook her head, her mouth tightening slightly. 'The first time he even held my hand you appeared and sent him packing, and he was too offended or inhibited or something ever to make another move with me again.'

'You must have had boyfriends in Australia?' Simon prompted urgently, ignoring the reproach.

'Boyfriends, not lovers.' Fee saw his blank incomprehension and it broke her heart. 'You can't understand that, can you? I wanted—I didn't want to live like nearly everyone I know, playing at love. Oh, I know how naïve it sounds, and maybe it's not realistic at all, but it's how I am...or how I was, because—I don't know what you've done to me, Simon. I keep thinking maybe, just maybe, I could give up wanting old-fashioned things, and be with you, because I want...what you want, if that's all I can have——'

And here she was, still stupidly hoping that he could reassure her and reduce his past, plus his enduring cynicism, to a size and shape she could deal with, because even if an affair couldn't make her truly happy it was what he wanted—for now—and she ached to make *him* happy, if only in the superficial way which was all he seemed capable of.

And here she was too having to fight back tears as she saw what was happening, the way his expression grew remote, and knew it for the withdrawal of his interest as he absorbed what he had just learned and *he* realised that she never could make him happy. She was too inexperienced; Fee could almost follow his thoughts despite the way he was masking them now.

So this was it at last, the abrupt loss of interest she had always been expecting, come too late for her to feel the relief she had once so confidently anticipated. Instead, Fee felt as if she was dying.

Already he was abandoning that carefully emotionless mask, boredom creeping into his expression as he leaned back, long legs stretched out in front of him, hands clasped behind his head.

Fee managed not to flinch as he glanced at her and she recognised a familiar ruthlessness in the tense curve of his mouth, but the indifference in his eyes seared her.

'Look, maybe you're right, Fee,' he agreed with an ennui to match the look in his eyes. 'The difficulties would seem to be insurmountable after all, since I can hardly rewrite my personal history, so perhaps we should just forget it.'

At least he wasn't making it as callous as his rejection of Ismay Compton all those years ago. He was actually ready to let her think he was seeing the issue from her point of view at last and that he accepted it.

But, perversely, Fee wasn't prepared to play it that way.

'It's because of what you've just found out, isn't it?' she challenged in a tight, hard voice. 'Because I've never had any real lovers.'

'Oh, that's a major part of it, admittedly,' he conceded dismissively. 'Initiating innocents has never been my scene.'

Fee shaped a mocking smile. 'I remember after you'd told Ismay Compton you didn't want her you said I should see you when I'd grown up and got a bit of experience. Should I still let you know when that happens?'

Simon's face tightened and he stirred irritably.

'I wouldn't rush into anything, sweetheart, and if you've managed to stay so completely innocent this long maybe you really are destined for those old-fashioned things you mentioned,' he advised, and gestured disgustedly. 'God, I shudder to think of what they might be... But I'd better go and leave you alone. You look terrible and I'd suggest an early night if you hope to be any use at the office tomorrow.'

'You wouldn't prefer a more experienced assistant?' Fee couldn't help herself.

'You're starting to bore me, Fee,' Simon snapped. 'Our private relationship hasn't intruded on our working one, so why should anything change now that we've decided to abandon the personal side?'

They had decided. Fee supposed it was accurate. She hadn't wanted an affair with Simon, and now he no longer wanted one either. She had no right to the misery clawing at her heart.

She put down her glass, feeling suddenly sick, and such was the distance between her and Simon now that neither of them spoke as she accompanied him to the door, shrugging out of his jacket and handing it to him.

'Thanks,' he said briefly.

He couldn't wait to get away from her, she accepted bitterly. He turned and strode away, disappearing from her view before she had even closed the door again.

It had finally happened. Simon had lost interest in her.

Only much later that night did she give way, weeping quietly and helplessly for the man she loved and the withdrawal of his shallow interest, once resented, now suddenly so much more desirable than his new indifference.

CHAPTER NINE

Now that Simon had lost interest in Fee as a woman, it was obvious that he no longer felt any incentive to show her the charming side of his nature which had caused so many women to forgive him so much over the years.

All week Fee suffered under both his natural impatience and an excessively edgy mood, his tolerance a thing of the past, replaced by a driving perfectionism and occasionally unreasonable demands.

'Didn't you once boast that you managed to stay friends with women after you lost interest in them?' she snapped unwisely one morning, goaded beyond endurance.

Simon went from furiously blazing irritation to icy rejection in the space of seconds.

'I'd appreciate it if you'd leave personal matters behind at home instead of dragging them into the office with you,' he requested coldly and watched with deliberate cruelty as she absorbed it. 'After all, you did insist that certain rules govern our working relationship. I merely pointed out that you were late.'

'Less than five minutes,' she offered, completely losing the remnants of an earlier urge to apologise.

'Why?'

'Because I overslept.' Her answer bordered on insolent.

And she had overslept because it had been three o'clock before any sleep had come to her in the first place.

Simon's mouth tightened, giving him an oddly nervy look as he stared at her.

'Maynah Norman was never late,' he said abruptly.

'Because she just couldn't wait to see you again every morning.' Fee knew it was a cheap crack and she dropped her eyes for a few seconds, drawing a slow, controlling breath before raising them to his angrily brooding face again. 'I suppose you're wishing you had her or someone else working for you now instead of me because you're feeling a fool, having thought you wanted me only to find you don't really after all, but stop taking it out on me, Simon. It's your responsibility; *you* decided you had to do Charles a favour and offer me this job.'

'I never feel a fool,' he retorted crushingly. 'May I remind you that you're here to work, not to attempt to analyse me? Plus you know me well enough to be aware that I was not doing Charles a favour. You got the job because you were capable of doing it, or so it seemed, but apparently the first flush of enthusiasm that made you so efficient is fading... And don't wear that perfume in the office again. I don't like it.'

'I'm not wearing any.'

'Whatever it is, then.'

His mood continued to be unreasonable and he lost his temper quite spectacularly with a couple of people that week. Fee knew it was only a matter of time before she found herself the target of one of his sharp-tongued rages and she kept bracing herself mentally, warily alert every time his glance strayed her way, whether idly or deliberately.

She half expected the explosion to occur on the Friday morning when he was having one of his irregular meetings with Rhodes Properties' various departmental heads, including Miss Sung-Li from Personnel, in the small informal conference-room adjoining their suite of offices.

For a start, Simon was already offended by the head of Marketing, whose natural caution made him distrustful of the facts and figures he could reel off from memory, and he was terse as he demanded the document the man required as confirmation.

Self-consciously aware of everyone present watching her, and recognising the stormy look in Simon's eyes, Fee took extra care, double-checking the title and coding of the relevant segment although she had been prepared for the demand, nervous of making a mistake but equally apprehensive of his finding her caution unacceptably slow.

To her surprise, however, the explosion never came, although his mouth remained tight, so sheer relief caused her to relax her guard, and she was unprepared, the colour draining from her face as he turned on her after the meeting had ended and the others departed for their own offices.

'Perhaps you were right! I'm seriously beginning to regret letting Charles influence me, since apparently it's beyond you to supply what I require promptly...'

There was more, but afterwards she could never remember all that he had said, and she didn't really take it in at the time either. She just stood there, shrivelling under a corrosive cascade of criticism as he lashed her with his tongue, too devastated to summon any sort of defence, incapable of even the simple expedient of flight until a belated sense of her rights rescued her and anger rose.

'It hasn't taken you long to change your mind and start blaming Charles, considering that only a day or two ago you were still denying that you'd offered me this job as a favour to him—but that's absolutely typical of how perverse you've been all week,' she taunted cuttingly. 'This—now—is just another example of that! Why didn't you say all this at the time, when I was being insufficiently prompt for your liking, and I could have speeded it up, instead of waiting until now——?'

'Because I happen to know how you fall apart when you've got a whole lot of people staring at you, especially in uncomfortable circumstances,' he derided bitingly.

It silenced Fee. She wanted to weep, unbearably moved by this unexpected evidence of the obvious strength of mind or character that had enabled him to remember and consider that personal idiosyncrasy of hers even while he was in a blazing temper. Her eyes focused on the toes of his expensive leather shoes as she tried to assemble a professionally composed expression.

'I'm sorry I was slow,' she began finally, looking up, but then personal resentment mastered her once more. 'You made me nervous.'

'Then you're not fit to be doing this job,' Simon returned, brutally dismissive as he glanced at his watch. 'I have to go over to the New Territories. I'll be quite late getting back, but there's nothing I'll want you for, so don't wait. I'll see you on Monday.'

He was right, Fee reflected unhappily when he had gone. Loving Simon made her unfit to be his assistant because she was incapable of keeping her own rules. Emotion got in the way. It wasn't the hard, impatient side of his nature that was affecting her, though; it was the little instances of caring, such as his consideration for her hatred of attention; the glimpses of the man he could be—the man she loved—that made it unbearable to go on working for him.

'Yes, it might be possible for you to swap jobs with . . . let's see, the head of Services' assistant, I think,' Miss Sung-Li conceded disapprovingly when Fee went to see her. 'But put your request for a transfer in writing, to Mr Rhodes and to me, and then if he's willing we'll see what can be done. If, as you imply, a personality clash has emerged, he may be agreeable, although he won't be too pleased at having to get used to yet another assistant.'

Simon hadn't returned to the office by the time she was ready to leave, so Fee left his copy of her request on his desk and went home to change, having promised to attend one of Babs's dinner parties that night. She didn't feel like socialising, but for Babs's sake, because she had been so concerned about her since discovering that she was in love with Simon, she was determined to make a show of philosophical insouciance. For her own sake, too. She couldn't let this crush her.

She arrived at the house early, but Babs, still wandering around in a robe, claimed not to need any help and left her downstairs.

'Charles is showering and I must dress. If anyone else arrives, let them in, give them a drink and entertain them ... on the patio as it's a nice evening. You look gorgeous, little one, only you could do with more make-up, blusher especially,' she added before disappearing upstairs.

The doorbell rang only a few minutes later, and Fee's determined composure shattered as she pulled open the front door and found Simon standing there, still in the clothes he had worn at work although he was carrying his jacket and his tie was loosened, the top buttons of his shirt undone, its sleeves rolled up.

For the most fleeting of moments her reaction to his presence was the familiar one—that coming to life, so vibrant and intense that soft warm colour flooded her face. Then in the next second it had receded, leaving her even paler than before.

'What do you want?' she demanded, the hostile tone deliberately contrived, because all she could feel was love and the pain of longing. 'Babs and Charles are having a dinner party, but I happen to know you're not invited.'

She had made sure of that before agreeing to attend.

'I want to talk to you, obviously,' Simon answered her impatiently. 'You weren't at your apartment and this seemed the obvious place to try next.'

Fee drew a sharp breath, one hand playing nervously with the door-handle.

'Anything you've got to say to me can be said at Rhodes Properties. That's the only relationship we've got these days,' she added a little bitterly.

'This is to do with our working relationship, but since you weren't *at* the office...' Simon shrugged. 'I want to know the meaning of that ridiculous request I found on my desk.'

'Couldn't you understand it?' Fee mocked. 'I thought I'd used absolutely plain English. I want to move to one of the regular departments.'

'Yes, but why? Because I bawled you out today? You can take it, Fee.' He paused, hard blue eyes sweeping her outfit of a plain strapless black top and graceful black lace skirt of mid-calf length, a recent purchase from Stanley Market. 'You're tougher than you think.'

'It has nothing to do with that,' Fee denied the charge, taking a hasty step backwards as he moved into the hallway. 'I really don't think you should come in, Simon. Babs doesn't like you any more.'

'I don't particularly like her either,' he returned dismissively, the hand he had put out to her bare shoulder swiftly removed and then returned to where the soft fabric of her top covered her lower back as he turned her towards the lounge door. 'In here. Then what is it about if not that? You said I made you nervous, I remember... But you had, and have, no need to be. You ought to have known that—known that I'd never embarrass you by criticising you in front of other people. You might have had that much faith in me. You can trust me, Fee.'

In the lounge, Fee faced him.

'When not so long ago you said I trust too much?' she challenged sharply. 'And you were right. Why should I trust you now?'

'Because in this matter you can—because you know me.' His confidence was almost arrogance.

'Why even in this matter?' she taunted sceptically. 'Four years ago, you didn't feel any compunction about humiliating me publicly——'

'Forget that,' Simon snapped irritably. 'There was a reason for the way I behaved then, but I will never treat you like that again, Fee, so there's no need for you to request a move.'

Fee shook her head helplessly, watching him drop his jacket on to a chair.

'Except that my request has nothing to do with that either,' she asserted tightly, and saw him frown. 'Don't you know what it is really, Simon? With all your experience, you ought to have guessed!'

Had she really once complacently congratulated herself because she wasn't going to end up like Maynah Norman?

'I do know that you're letting something emotional get in the way,' Simon stated grimly. 'Not very professional of you, is it, Fee?'

'Probably not,' she acknowledged caustically. 'But you see, Simon, I'm putting myself first—my *emotional* self, because I am an *emotional* being . . . You wouldn't have a clue about that, though, would you? But there are a lot of us around, you know, people whose work— careers—are important to them, yes, but who aren't obsessed the way you are, because they've got other things they value in their lives . . . like peace, and emotional and mental comfort. But I don't expect you to understand, because Rhodes Properties is all you care about really.'

'Or all I've got?' he suggested tautly.

'The only thing of value anyway, because it's the only thing you find fulfilling,' she derided.

'Yes, you may be right there,' he allowed, unusually harsh. 'But that's beside the point——'

'I'm not withdrawing my request,' she insisted swiftly. 'And if you can't or won't grant it, I'll just have to leave Rhodes Properties altogether. I'm sorry to be messing you around like this, but it's just not working out, and I have to consider myself.'

Simon was silent for so long that at first Fee thought he must be concocting some ploy to manipulate her into changing her mind and thus spare himself the annoyance of having to adjust to yet another assistant. Then she became aware of his complicated expression, as if he was conducting some internal debate with himself.

'I suppose I've messed you around equally,' he said finally in a voice so empty of any sort of emotion that Fee had a strong sense of some kind of struggle being at an end. 'Will you really be happier away from me, child?'

Child. Fee had frozen. So it had come to this. In Simon's eyes she had become a child, divested of her womanhood by his discovery that she had never had a lover.

'Yes!' It was emphatic, but inwardly she was falling apart.

Simon stirred restlessly, taking a step towards her, lifting his hands but letting them drop again without touching her.

'And are you so very unhappy now, little Fee?' he asked, expression returning to his voice, but the tone was so gently indulgent that even without the inaccurate adjective preceding her name it would have put him firmly in the same camp as those others, like Babs, to whom she had remained 'little Fee'.

'Yes!' Suddenly beyond dissembling, feeling as if she was dying, Fee confirmed it despairingly and, since he couldn't bring himself to touch her, some treacherous, self-destructive instinct made her move forward and lift her hands to his shoulders, utterly unable to help herself. 'You know what's happened, don't you? I should hate you for it, only I can't! *I love you!*'

Simon was standing very still. He had put his arms round her, apparently instinctively, but the part of her which accepted that he could never love her observed that he was careful to keep his hands from touching her bare shoulders—probably as a result of years of experience in trying not to excite the ardour of scores of importunate lovelorn women, she reflected bleakly.

'I know you do, but you must realise that I cannot accept your love, sweetheart.' He rejected her as if it was a set speech, often used, which it probably was.

'And yet you thought you wanted me before,' she reminded him ironically.

'I know. As I say, I'm fully aware that I've messed you around.' His tone was harder now, and almost indifferent. 'But, as we agreed, there was too much in the way.'

Fee broke away from him then, her colour high as she realised how fully she had revealed herself, actually inviting—forcing—his explicit rejection, so superfluous when she already knew he no longer wanted her and could never love her. He had sounded so bored. Why not? How many other women had he had to discourage once he found he no longer wanted them?

'I'm sorry if I've embarrassed you, but you must be used to it,' she offered sardonically, an aching dignity in the way she lifted her chin and met his eyes. 'I'm just like Maynah Norman and all the others, aren't I?'

'No. No, you are not.'

Simon spoke with a tightness that suggested controlled anger and, noticing his strained expression, Fee felt guilty.

'I suppose you think I've got no pride,' she guessed savagely to cover it.

'No, I just think you're incapable of pretence,' he responded colourlessly.

Anger added itself to her distress as she began to realise what a fool she had just made of herself, telling him she loved him, although it seemed that he had already known that—and again, why not? He was so used to being loved by multitudes of women, and, while he might welcome it from some, not even he could possibly want all the women who loved him.

'I must compliment you on how well you do this, even managing to sound kind!' She flung it at him mockingly. 'But then, you must have lots of practice in turning us down——'

She broke off as the phone beside her rang, reaching for it automatically, too devastated emotionally to remember the rule about not answering calls when she was in this house.

'Wait, Fee, let me. Don't——' Simon halted as she gave the number.

Once again the slight delay told her it was an international call, but she was still disorientated, only tensing and her eyes flying helplessly to Simon's face as she heard Vance Sheldon begin, 'So you're there for once, are you? Now listen to me; after the exhibition you made of me and yourself in Perth, you owe it to me——'

That was all she heard as Simon put out a hand, breaking the connection with a stab of his finger, then taking the receiver from her and putting it down next to the phone.

'Why did you answer?' he demanded impatiently. 'It was Sheldon, wasn't it? Still trying to bully you into returning?'

'Yes. I wasn't thinking...' Fee shook her head unhappily.

His exasperation fading, Simon stared at her for a moment before pulling her into his arms.

'Poor baby,' he murmured roughly against her hair.

Baby now. Fee absorbed it anguishedly but stayed where she was. Hearing Vance Sheldon's voice hadn't upset her nearly as much this time, mainly because she had too much personal and immediate distress to contend with, the reality of Simon and his rejection of her making everything else seem slightly unreal in comparison, and definitely unimportant. Mr Sheldon now seemed slightly ridiculous, and mere harassment could never hurt again, now that she knew what real hurt was.

But if this was the only way she could be in Simon's arms, probably for the last time ever, then she was content to let him believe that she was distraught over the call.

Fee clung to him, shaking with yearning, her heart bursting with love. She could feel Simon's fingers moving soothingly in her curls as she dropped her head to his shoulder, then spreading out to cradle the back of her skull, pressing her even closer. His other hand was at her back, moving slowly up beneath the loose fall of her satiny hair and coming to rest between her shoulders, fingers rubbing gently at the smooth bare skin, back and forth and up and down.

She was melting, and yet shattering too at the same time somehow, simply dissolving with love and breaking apart with the knowledge that he no longer wanted her. Unmoving save for those magical hands, he stood so still, a man doing his duty as common humanity demanded, offering comfort but unstirred by desire, let alone love——

And she loved him so much! A tiny moan of agony and despair escaped her and she raised her head anxiously, looking into his face and searching it urgently, but, while Simon's eyes were open, they looked like a blind man's, unseeing though they stared into hers. Hope and desperation died. She couldn't make him love her, so what use was it to beg, to plead, to demand, as she had been about to do despite everything she already knew, including the fact that hope was futile? He had heard it all before, from so many like her, and why should his reaction be any different this time? She was just one of the crowd.

'God, it makes me sick, the way history has to repeat itself.' Simon sounded savagely disgusted as he released her abruptly. 'I've never really believed in the concept of inescapable destiny, but it seems I was wrong. Damn you, Fee.'

It was one of anger's betrayals, the truth spoken unthinkingly. Despite his earlier denial, Simon did see her as being just like Maynah and all the other women who had loved him—and undoubtedly despised her for it.

'Am I supposed to apologise?' she flared furiously, her own anger arising out of humiliation.

Simon was white with rage, his eyes stormy, and she saw him literally bite back whatever he had been about to say. After a few tense seconds, he succeeded in looking merely irritable, his lips curving derisively.

'Not you, Fee,' he murmured drily, before becoming decisive. 'Where's Charles? Find him and tell him I want to see him—and try to keep that stepsister of yours away if you possibly can.'

'I'm supposed to give their guests drinks and entertain them on the patio if they arrive,' Fee remembered. 'I thought it was some of them when you rang the doorbell.'

'I'll stand in for you while you find Charles,' he offered impatiently, clearly still working off some excess anger or frustration. 'Go on, Fee.'

He was probably sick of the mere sight of her, just one more among all the legions of languishing women in whom he had lost interest, Fee reflected savagely, but she moved to do as she was bid, needing to get away from him now, embarrassment beginning to set in.

Since she had never done such a thing before, Charles looked startled when she knocked on the door of his and Babs's bedroom, once too briefly and rarely shared by Jim and Angela.

'She's in the bathroom,' he told her.

'Not her—you,' Fee corrected his misapprehension. 'Simon is downstairs. He wants to see you.'

'Oh? Was it he who answered that phone call, by the way? He was too quick for Babs or me to get to the phone in here, but I presume it wasn't for us anyway?'

'I answered it by mistake. It was Mr Sheldon.'

Charles was galvanised into action, swearing indignantly and bounding out of the room.

'Charlie? What's wrong?' Babs's muffled voice came from the bathroom.

'Nothing serious, Babs,' Fee called, and slipped away before more difficult questions were asked.

She sat in her own old bedroom for a while, trying to assemble the composure she would need to get her through the evening, only going downstairs again after she had heard Babs do so in response to the sound of people arriving below.

She heard Charles speaking in the lounge, but Babs and most of the guests must be out on the patio, she thought, hesitating in the hallway.

She was about to enter and go through when she heard Charles saying regretfully, 'No, on second thoughts I agree with you, Simon; we can't ask her to do that. But as for your suggestion, I'd take that on myself with the greatest of pleasure——'

'No, that's my prerogative, Charles,' Simon cut in with typical arrogance.

She couldn't face him again, not so soon after he had rejected her and killed the last of the hope she hadn't even known she held, hope to which she had had no right, Fee thought frantically, turning away and heading for the kitchen instead.

She was opening a bottle of mineral water when Simon found her.

'Charles may get the number here changed, but, if he doesn't, just remember never to answer the phone when you're visiting. That way you won't have to worry about Sheldon,' he told her abruptly. 'I just wanted to remind you before I left.'

'Yes.' Once Fee would have been furious with him for interfering, and with both men for discussing the matter without consulting her, but now she couldn't even look at him, let alone summon any anger. 'Thank you.'

'Charles invited me to stay for dinner but I didn't think you'd appreciate it, and neither would Babs, judging by the frozen greeting she gave me,' he went on ironically, then sighed when she made no response. 'All right, Fee, I'll tell Miss Sung-Li you're to be transferred to Services on Monday if that's really what you want. As for the other thing, it would never have worked . . . you and me. I'd only have made you very unhappy.'

'I know you would,' she acknowledged acidly.

'Yes, that's why you want this transfer, isn't it? Because you can't obey your own rules any longer. So perhaps it's for the best after all,' he conceded harshly.

Then he had gone and Fee buried her face in her hands, wondering how she was ever going to survive the anguish that was tearing her apart.

*   *   *

Fee's new boss was a reserved but easygoing man with little to say for himself and a merciful and total absence of curiosity about her as a person, but he seemed to find her work satisfactory, thanking her with grave courtesy for everything she did.

Now that she was no longer Simon's personal assistant, her fellow-employees clearly felt no obligation to cease abruptly any Simon-related gossip and speculation whenever she appeared, and she heard two junior secretaries talking avidly about him as they walked just ahead of her through the building's underground parking area at the end of Wednesday.

'No, I have it on good authority that it's not a business trip,' one was asserting confidently. 'So it must be a holiday—somewhere exotic, I bet. Maybe it's to get over whatever's been bugging him lately! I wonder who he's taken with him?'

'I haven't heard of anyone new since he ditched Loren Kincaid, have you? But he'll pick someone up, that's for sure.'

Fee ached, but she couldn't feel angry. Simon had earned his reputation.

But tormenting visions of him on some glamorous beach, always with a woman, haunted her nights, and the days were as bad. One man had absented himself, and teeming Hong Kong felt empty and dead.

Babs was still almost oppressively anxious about her emotional well-being, and in her present state of mind Fee found it easier to give in to her insistence that she needed company, rather than enduring constant phone calls, so she was with her and Charles the following Sunday morning, lounging beside their swimming-pool and reading a serious newspaper article about the refugee problem when Babs squeaked and looked up from her more sensational section of the paper.

'I do not believe this! Simon Rhodes has been charged with assault! In Australia!' Her voice swooped upwards. 'It says... Oh, yes, he simply hit the guy once. "Rhodes Properties in Hong Kong...incident took place...business premises of famous financier Vance Sheldon"... *Vance Sheldon*, Fee!'

Charles snatched the paper away from his wife.

'My God, he actually went and did it. I thought it was just talk... Last time Sheldon phoned, Simon and I discussed what to do about it, how to stop him. He said he'd like to get his hands on the swine and I agreed; I offered to do it but I'm sorry to have to confess that I wasn't exactly serious... but Simon said it was his right or some such thing. Obviously *he* was serious.' Charles looked at Fee with sudden respect. 'Hell, Fee!'

Fee was silent, waiting her turn and reading the story for herself, but she learnt no more than Babs had already announced. Simon had gone to Australia and thrown a punch at Vance Sheldon.

'I can't get over it!' Charles was inclined to find it funny. 'Simon, stirring himself on someone else's behalf. That's a first!'

Fee couldn't say a word. She just sat there, thinking and thinking about what Simon had done, her mind testing what intuition was telling her about the reason for his action.

After a while Charles went indoors, but Babs remained sitting on the edge of her sun-lounger, initially as silent as Fee.

Eventually, though, she stirred and prompted, 'Fee?'

Fee looked up and Babs caught her breath as she saw her expression.

'He does care about me,' Fee said in a soft, shaky voice.

'Oh, darling, you mustn't read too much into it,' Babs cautioned her urgently. 'You've said yourself that he's lost interest in you. You heard what Charles said—that the two of them discussed it together; you're like some child we all love, and they wanted to protect you from that monster... Simon acted for us all.'

Fee shook her head. 'When I really was a child, Simon would never have done anything like this for me, and he doesn't do things like that for anyone, anyway. He simply doesn't care enough usually. That's what Charles meant a few minutes ago. Oh, Babs!'

'Fee, you can't know!' Babs sounded almost frantic. 'It was probably an impulse, it doesn't mean anything, and you're going to get your heart broken all over again if you start getting your hopes up like this.'

'I can know, because it's so untypical of Simon generally, so utterly pointless and...and ridiculously quixotic. I'm not——' Fee broke off, but her eyes were still soft and shining. 'I'm not saying he has suddenly fallen in love with me or anything dramatic like that, but he does care about me, and I think he might even still want me. There've been other little things, a way of considering me personally. I didn't think it meant anything, but now I don't know, because it was also untypical of him. When he comes back, if he wants me, then I'm going to...I don't know...be what he wants me to be. I'll ask him——'

'Oh, Fee, I'm so afraid for you,' Babs confessed feelingly as Fee broke off emotionally.

'So am I,' Fee admitted shakily. 'But I have to find out.'

'And nothing I can say will stop you, will it?' Babs accepted.

'No,' Fee confirmed.

CHAPTER TEN

A TINY paragraph in one of the evening newspapers the following week announced that the charge against Simon Rhodes had been dropped. No explanation was given.

But Simon hadn't returned to Hong Kong. Fee knew that because everyone was talking about him at work but no one had seen him. Sunday's story was responsible for endless speculation, the consensus of opinion being that such behaviour was uncharacteristic of Simon; someone remembered that Vance Sheldon had featured in an even more sensational story not long ago, the details were recalled, and Fee found herself the subject of much curious gossip. As always, she shrank sensitively from the attention of strangers, but at the same time there was a new, tender warmth around her heart. Simon had done it for her, and she couldn't help being moved and a little proud.

She knew now that he cared about her in some unusual and sensitive way. What she didn't know was if he had meant his rejection because he had genuinely lost interest in her after discovering how inexperienced she was, or whether all his recent moody irritability had been because he still secretly wanted her but had decided that he couldn't have her for some reason.

Fee wasn't confident enough to make any easy assumptions, but she wondered constantly, and even if he sincerely didn't want her his caring was special and she would always treasure it.

She was anxious for his return, needing the mystery solved, her confidence waning when there was no news of him, and she was eventually driven to risk exciting further speculation by ringing through to his office and asking when he was due back, but her replacement said she hadn't heard from him.

It was Saturday morning when she finally learned of his return from a morning newspaper, one of the sober ones, so it merely stated that Simon had declined to comment on what it called the fracas in Sydney on his return to Hong Kong the previous evening.

Suddenly Fee was more frightened than she had ever been in her life, and by the time she drove up to the gates of Simon's house on the Peak she was pale with nerves, her hands clammy on the steering-wheel. But she had to know.

At the entrance, she encountered a problem. Since she wasn't expected, Mr Deng claimed to have no authority to admit her.

'At least tell Mr Rhodes I'm here and see what he says,' Fee beseeched him urgently, embarrassed by his cynical expression and wondering how many times he had turned other uninvited women away from these same gates in the past, but too desperate to be deterred. 'He *might* want to see me.'

Apparently he did, because after using the intercom system Mr Deng allowed the gates to glide open and she drove in.

The main door to the house opened as she got out of the car unsteadily, discovering that her legs were suddenly shaking so badly that she could barely stand.

The shirt Simon wore with his jeans hadn't been tucked in or buttoned, and Fee looked up at him as he came to stand at the top of the stairs, her attempted smile a shaky failure.

'Were you just getting up? I'm sorry, I didn't think,' she apologised breathlessly, and in the next instant the appalling possibility that he might not have been getting up alone slammed into her heart and mind.

He didn't move.

'Are you going to start making a nuisance of yourself, Fee?' he enquired unpleasantly, giving her a twisted smile. 'I told Deng he could let you in because I knew it would embarrass you to have him turn you away, but that's as much as I can do for you. For the last time, I am no longer interested in having an affair with you, and perhaps it's time you cultivated some pride after all, if you can't control your feelings. I had hoped last time was a one-off lapse, due to the heat of the moment.'

Humiliated, she dropped her gaze, and was on the point of fleeing, but then anger rose.

'What are you interested in, then, Simon?' she asked softly, approaching the stairs.

'Not you, anyway, so don't bother coming up,' he advised her brutally.

Fee was trembling from head to foot, but she still started up the stairs.

'Then I won't bother you again,' she promised him bitterly. 'But I would like to... thank you for what you did. In Australia.'

An exasperated sigh escaped him. 'Oh, yes, the Press couldn't resist it, could they? If I'd merely done what I went there to do, there'd have been no charge, no consequent attention... Oh, come on up, then, and I'll tell you what it was about, but then I want you out of here.'

He looked exhausted, Fee noticed as she reached him and he drew back to let her precede him into the house as if making sure she had no opportunity to touch him. His tan seemed to have faded, faint bruise-coloured smudges lay under his eyes and the tension about his mouth gave him a harsh, slightly haggard look.

But his eyes themselves were hard and cool with rejection, and she shivered slightly under the cursory inspection they gave her face and ultra-slender figure simply clad in jeans and her favourite loose black T-shirt.

'Here?' she questioned, hesitating at a door, and Simon nodded briefly, following her in.

The lounge was a long, beautiful room, its décor all light elegant colours, a few pieces of Chinese jade and the books, video cassettes and compact discs crowding some substantial shelving providing character.

'Yes, you're entitled to know that you don't need to worry about Sheldon ever again,' Simon allowed decisively as she turned to face him. 'I was going to get Charles to tell you. Additionally, if you like, you could have recourse to various restraining orders, possibly even charges, although defining the nature of his calls might cause problems; for instance, did he ever actually threaten you, or was it pure harassment—persecution? Anyway, as far as a charge goes, it would have to apply to those you received before you left Australia. But that's one of the things I went there to look into, because Charles's original idea, if a charge *was* possible, to get you to take one of the calls and listen long enough to get a decent recording for a voice-print ID would have been too upsetting for you, and he had taken to hanging up if Charles or Babs answered. Plus I assumed, rightly, I hope, that you wouldn't actually want to go ahead with anything that would attract publicity, but I needed to show Sheldon that you could, and that you would if he didn't stop. That's it, really, except that when I went to see him I looked at him and all I could think of was what he'd tried to do to you, all I could see was you, standing there listening to him when he rang, so I hit him.'

'For me.' Fee's eyes searched his face, but it didn't soften.

Simon shrugged. 'He deserved it, although I shouldn't have done it, but I think I always subconsciously meant to... He found the authorities unsympathetic. They knew why I'd done it, and they let him know how much I'd given them concerning those calls and hinted that I'd prove vindictive, perhaps go to the Press, if he went ahead with the assault charge. He's not a popular man. It wasn't a deal, just Sheldon showing some signs of sense and self-preservation. Now that he realises just how much is known by how many people, he'll be too busy patching up his reputation to risk bothering you again.'

'I'm glad. Simon...' Fee put out a shaky hand but he ignored it.

'Now will you please leave, Fee?' he demanded bitingly.

'Yes.' She knew she would have to, and tears stood in her eyes. 'It was nice of you to care, and to take the trouble, because you don't usually, do you? That's why I thought you might...still want me.'

Simon's face tightened.

'I do not want to have an affair with you,' he enunciated slowly, clearly near the end of his tolerance.

It made all her other unanswered questions irrelevant, and she averted her gaze.

'Then...just thank you,' she whispered chokily as she began to move past him. 'I'm sorry to have...bothered you—I'll always love you!'

She just couldn't help herself.

'And what about my past?' Simon retorted with caustic derision. 'Not to mention all your little comments to the effect that I'm too old for you? You've changed your tune lately, haven't you?'

'I don't care about your previous lovers any more. And you were right that time you said you were the perfect age for me. You're the one who has changed,' she countered accusingly.

Simon's fists were clenched at his sides and he flung his head up, staring hard at the ceiling for a moment.

'Because, once and for all, Fee, I am no longer interested in getting you into my bed. What does it take to put you off?' he demanded cruelly, and winced slightly as he saw her lips quiver. 'Don't look like that! Damn it, how do you think I feel when you come here, and look at me, and say things——?'

'Now you know how I used to feel, when you first started this whole business,' she flared resentfully, out of an unbelievable depth of pain, 'before I knew I loved you, and before you changed your mind.'

'Yes, I should never have begun it, I should never have let myself be attracted to you, because by the time I realised it had no future it was too late for you, wasn't it? And if you won't leave me alone, if you're going to haunt me like this... how the hell am I going to go on resisting you?'

A jolt of comprehension drove the breath from her lungs as she absorbed what he had just said, and it was several seconds before she could speak.

'What do you have to resist if you don't want to have an affair with me any more?' she asked in a small quavery voice, suddenly afraid of hope.

'The temptation to make you—to ask you to marry me!' Simon lost control of his temper with characteristic suddenness. 'To ask you to let me give you all those old-fashioned things you want, to stay with me all our lives, and be there always, and make a family with me, and all the things I never thought I wanted and now when I do I can't have them. I can't have an affair with you now, and I can't marry you either because how could you ever be happy and secure, knowing me as you do, knowing what I've been like all my life...? Oh, God, Fee, what are you doing to me now?'

She had come to him, her hands clutching instinctively at his upper arms as she stared at him in absolute astonishment.

'Simon, you said people shouldn't get married. You've said it twice that I remember,' she recalled, her voice cracking.

'Oh, Fee, I thought I knew it all, didn't I?' Simon groaned. 'I didn't believe in marriage because I'd seen too many marriages failing, but I've realised lately that the people concerned either didn't love or else didn't know *how* to love properly. You do know how to love, and now I do too—— Don't touch me, darling. It nearly killed me to have you in my arms last time and to have to pretend——'

'I want to, and I don't want you to pretend anything,' Fee insisted unsteadily. 'But you don't have to marry me, Simon.'

'I know, I can't, but I can't bear anything less. It would be too easy for you to get away from me when I made you miserable, and you started wondering if I was being faithful... And how could you ever *know*?' he concluded in an intense whisper.

'Just because I do know you. You couldn't change like this and want such things if it wasn't something drastic...'

Fee's voice faded away as she absorbed the magnitude of the change in him, and awe crept into her gaze as she went on staring at him.

Simon gave a faint uneven laugh and she was aware of a slight tremor in his hands as they came to rest at her waist.

'Oh, it's drastic, which makes the way it all crept up on me highly ironic—and it has happened twice over. I couldn't believe it when I had to give you up all over again. You see, it was always there. There were things, feelings I'd deliberately put out of my mind the first time around because I knew they had no future. I remember coming across you holding hands with Warren Bates years and years ago, and feeling as if the ground had collapsed under my feet. I knew I couldn't have you, you were too young to have handled what I felt for you, so I convinced myself that you were too young to have a relationship with him either.

'In fact, the way I behaved then was sheer jealousy. It was on the same occasion that you tipped your drink all over me and ended up in my lap, and I found myself wanting to keep you there and hold on to you, and take you away with me and look after you. That's why I was so vile. It was a kind of defence; I was so afraid of being tempted to take advantage of you, especially as you were such a kind child, and terrified of revealing what I was feeling, because I suspected you'd find it too disturbing to deal with. You were so vulnerable... Oh, I didn't think what I was feeling amounted to anything more than the usual sort of attraction I went in for, my darling, but I knew I couldn't follow it up for your sake, that I had to bury it.

'It was only later, analysing it, that I realised it was more than attraction, that if I could bring myself to consider you at all and suppress my own selfish inclinations...then I *adored* you, Fee. It was the second hardest thing I've ever had to do in my life, letting you go, accepting that you'd probably meet and marry some nice young man in Australia. I didn't expect you to come back. But you did, with that sensual way of moving, a softly sophisticated image and a way of standing up for yourself that seemed to suggest you could take care of yourself these days; and with an affair with Sheldon behind you—as I thought.

'So it appeared that you were no more an idealist than I was now, that you enjoyed playing at love, the way I did, so I thought I'd like to have you in my life for a

while, my next affair. Only I kept catching myself acting
out of character, trying to be much nicer than I really
am, partly because I wanted you to think well of me,
but also simply wanting to take care of you and not hurt
you in any way—because I think I must have sensed how
vulnerable you really still were.

'I kept seeing beyond the sophisticated façade,
glimpsing the reality, but I suppressed my suspicions
every single time they were aroused. As it is, I should
have known for sure, I should have guessed at once.
There were so many clues—for instance, the fact that
you regarded me as old! That made you very young...
I think I probably *did* know when you told me the truth
about Sheldon when we were in Macau, but again I deliberately ignored it. I didn't want to believe it and have
to give you up a second time over.

'But I couldn't go on kidding myself any longer once
you'd told me the truth about yourself in so many words.
That hit me badly because I only fully recognised and
accepted what I was feeling for what it was when you
told me you'd never had any lovers at all. I suddenly
saw myself as another Sheldon, a selfish would-be seducer of innocents if I took advantage of what I knew
you were feeling, and I knew I could have had you then...
I had to be strong for both of us, and God, it was
difficult!'

'But if you'd told me what you really felt?' Fee
prompted gently as he fell silent, his face set in taut lines
of regret, and her heart could hardly contain the joy of
knowing that punching Vance Sheldon was only the least
of the things he had done for her sake, because there
had also been the self-denial, the sacrifices she had believed him incapable of. 'This time, anyway, because I
think you were right four years ago—I wouldn't have
known how to deal with it. But now... I would have

known you weren't taking advantage then, but by the end I wouldn't have really cared if you were, you know.'

'I do know. You never expected or asked for any equal return of your love, did you?' Simon closed his eyes momentarily as a spasm of emotion shook him. 'You're so undemanding and I'm so selfish, but I do love you, Fee.'

'I know you do.' She slipped her arms round him happily. 'But I wish I'd known before.'

'How could you when I was having such a hard time accepting it myself? And when I did—oh, Fee, you might have laughed at what I went through if you weren't too kind. A lot of people I know would definitely have laughed, and I'd deserve it,' he acknowledged with a slightly tired smile. 'The great intellect, wriggling and writhing in search of solutions. Your innocence confused me even more because it seemed that Babs and the others who treated you as a child must be right after all, and yet my sense of you was as a woman, and the woman I love and desire. I knew I couldn't have my usual kind of affair with you, but I didn't know what I could have. I'd never seen myself as a husband, faithful to one woman. It just never occurred to me for a while, and when it did I knew it would be no good for you.

'That's why I was so foul-tempered; when I still believed we were going to have an affair, I could be patient, because I was so sure of you, but without any hope whatsoever... I couldn't ask you to marry me; I still know I shouldn't, but I can't take any more, Fee. If you're brave enough to risk it, I think I'm desperate enough to let you.'

Starry-eyed, she laughed shakily as she held him tight with trembling arms.

'It hasn't got anything to do with bravery. Cowardice is more like it because I don't think I can live my life properly without you—and why should I have to when

you'll love me and understand me and look after me so
well?' she concluded on a note of rising confidence.

'Oh, Fee, you don't know——' Simon broke off,
clearly still struggling.

'But I do know,' she contradicted him tenderly and
saw his tense expression relax into a smile. 'And you
said it yourself just now, Simon—I also know how to
love.'

'Yes, you do!' he realised elatedly. 'You're the one
with all the understanding.'

'Is it so very hard to give up your freedom?' she went
on mischievously.

'It was never freedom,' Simon admitted slowly, his
arms closing round her.

'Could you kiss me, then?' she invited him, and after
an infinitesimal hesitation he did so, with a depth and
tenderness that made her heart stop and then race.

'What is it?' he asked concernedly as he raised his
head, because suddenly she was shaking violently, overwhelmed by reality's impact.

'It just seems so incredible...that you should love me,
and like this!' she confided brokenly, her bright lips
trembling. 'Simon, I'm not clever *or* stupid enough for
you.'

'You're perfect,' he reassured her. 'That's one of the
things I've always known—that that inane standard of
mine just didn't apply where you were concerned.'

'Then...Simon, I want, I need...Oh, I don't know
how to ask you,' she confessed and was stopped by his
thumb brushing across her mouth as he took her face
between his hands.

'Are you sure, Fee?' he questioned her tenderly. 'I can
wait now that I know you're going to be mine.'

Fee shook her head.

'I'm not a child!' she asserted passionately.

'I know, you're a lovely, loving, sensitive woman, as I always knew in my heart until the fact of your innocence got me so confused... And my woman,' Simon added with a touch of proud possessiveness, and paused, studying her still uncertain expression for a moment before she saw him make up his mind. 'But it happens quite naturally, Fee. Trust me, my darling; you really can this time.'

It did and she could, and much later that day, when neither of them had any doubts left about either each other or themselves, Fee smiled rapturously, eyes resting adoringly on the bright head that lay against her breasts. Simon had loved her with such passionate tenderness, and he had told her things so personal and private that she knew she had his heart in her safekeeping as surely as he had hers, and that their life together would be one of mutual cherishing.

'You're amazing,' she murmured simply and he raised his head, smiling down into her delicately flushed face, his eyes mirroring the love-languor in hers.

'And I worship you,' he offered seriously in return. 'I never want to be apart from you, not for a minute... When I thought I couldn't have you, I consoled myself that at least I'd have your presence, at the office, but then you asked to be transferred. I was all set to refuse, but then it occurred to me that once again I'd be behaving like Sheldon, trying to force you to remain in a situation that made you miserable. Will you come and work for me again? At least until we have our children?'

Fee laughed. 'If poor Miss Sung-Li will forgive us for messing her around one more time!'

'A lot of people are going to be annoyed for a variety of reasons,' he acknowledged wryly. 'Fee, I know you hate crowds of people looking at you, but can you bear a proper wedding? Now that I'm doing this, I need to do it thoroughly—I want everyone to know we belong together and be as sure as we are . . . Are you really going to marry me?'

'Really!'

'I'm actually getting married!'

He sounded so startled, but so pleased with himself at the same time that she hugged him.

In fact no one was annoyed although many were astonished when their wedding took place three weeks later, although Charles was slightly put out because he had wanted to give Fee away and Simon, with his gift for getting things done efficiently, had spoiled his fun by locating Jim Garland somewhere in the Karakoram and persuading him to come home; Angela too had been found and was rallying bravely after the news that an apprehensive but happy Babs was going to make her a grandmother in eight months' time, and she and Jim had decided to be friends for the day. Miss Sung-Li was beaming.

So everything was perfect, Fee reflected as she and Simon emerged from the church in which the ceremony had taken place, pausing for the photographers.

A pretty blonde girl in a short skirt went by on the other side of the road. Fee saw the idly appreciative look Simon sent after her and she couldn't hold back a gasp of laughter.

'She's gorgeous, isn't she?' she prompted.

'Is she? I didn't notice,' Simon returned blandly, and then he gave a shout of joyous, triumphant laughter as he lifted her high in the air so that the pleated silk of her skirt fanned out. 'No, there's only you now, and for always, my darling Fee.'

As he lowered her again, Fee was content. He might look, but he would never look at anyone else the way he was looking at her now, warm blue eyes ablaze with love.

Simon was Simon, and she loved him.

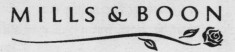

4 FREE

Romances and 2 FREE gifts just for you!

You can enjoy all the heartwarming emotion of true love for FREE! Discover the heartbreak and happiness, the emotion and the tenderness of the modern relationships in Mills & Boon Romances.

We'll send you 4 Romances as a special offer from Mills & Boon Reader Service, along with the opportunity to have 6 captivating new Romances delivered to your door each month.

Claim your FREE books and gifts overleaf...

An irresistible offer from Mills & Boon

Become a regular reader of Romances with Mills & Boon Reader Service and we'll welcome you with 4 books, a CUDDLY TEDDY and a special MYSTERY GIFT all absolutely FREE.

And then look forward to receiving 6 brand new Romances each month, delivered to your door hot off the presses, postage and packing FREE! Plus our free Newsletter featuring author news, competitions, special offers and much more.

This invitation comes with no strings attached. You may cancel or suspend your subscription at any time, and still keep your free books and gifts.

It's so easy. Send no money now. Simply fill in the coupon below and post it to -
Reader Service, FREEPOST, PO Box 236, Croydon, Surrey CR9 9EL.

- - - - **NO STAMP REQUIRED** - - - -

Free Books Coupon

Yes! Please rush me 4 FREE Romances and 2 FREE gifts! Please also reserve me a Reader Service subscription. If I decide to subscribe I can look forward to receiving 6 brand new Romances for just £10.80 each month, postage and packing FREE. If I decide not to subscribe I shall write to you within 10 days - I can keep the free books and gifts whatever I choose. I may cancel or suspend my subscription at any time. I am over 18 years of age.

Ms/Mrs/Miss/Mr _____ EP56R

Address _____

_____

Postcode _____ Signature _____

mps MAILING PREFERENCE SERVICE